THE MOON IN HABOCK'S MIRROR

THE MOON IN
HABOCK'S MIRROR

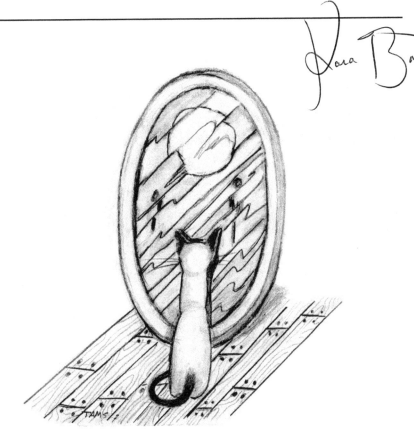

Kara Bartley

To order additional copies of this book, contact:
Xlibris Corporation
1-888-795-4274
www.Xlibris.com
Orders@Xlibris.com
123408

CONTENTS

For my parents who taught me the true value of time.
For Tammy, Ryan, Melissa and Jo Ann,
who supported me throughout this rollercoaster of a journey.
And to my furry little wise men who inspired the story:
Apollo, Achilles and Agamemnon
Without them, this tale could not be told.

PROLOGUE

Diary entry
December 7, 2012

I'm in desperate need of help—time is running out. I don't know what happened to me in the cave, but somehow I escaped the Mirrorwalkers. Thank God Sparks was there to find me. I'm home now but for how long? They said no matter where I hide, they'll find me and summon me to duty. I don't know what that means . . . and I'm scared.

I can feel their blackness spreading throughout my body, churning my blood. My heart is being torn in two directions; towards the path of strength and towards the path of weakness. The pull of evil is powerful and I can feel myself succumbing to their will more and more each day. Something dark is growing inside of me and the more I fight it, the more I sink. Soon they will find me, I just know it. What will they have me do?

Their Leader is coming, soon he will rise. They are preparing for his ascension on the 19th—the first night of the Spider moon. He will take the forests and set Blazenridge afire. Then he will head for Velvet Elm. Power over the Elms will signify our demise—I cannot let that happen!

The prophecy says 'One of strength to bind—two identical of power.' I know what that means but there must be another way. My sister can never know about this.

Avari has forsaken me, so I must do this without her light. Darkness will be my guide. I hope this book makes it safely to its destination—I guess only time will tell.

This plea for help will be my last, please help me if you can!

Scarlett Cavanaugh

IN LATE

Present Day
July, 2010

IN THESE LAST few years, I've learned that there are two ways to climb through a bedroom window. The first: a silent dismount onto the floor without any signs of detection; the second: a fumbling tumble as you lose your balance and land on something that shrieks—most likely a pet. Although the first scenario is the more coveted of the two, I have mastered both.

Tonight however, I was victorious. I was able to make it through the window and into my bed without as much as a peep from my shoes, the floor or the family dog.

As I slid beneath the sheets, I heard my twin sister, Gwendolyn, yawn. "You just getting in?"

I looked over at the bed next to me. "Yeah—Joel just dropped me off. Did Mom or Dad check in?"

"Nope, they went to bed early. Where'd you guys go tonight?" she asked.

"We went to Blue Beacon. The moon was bright and the stars were shining. Gweny—it was so beautiful."

I loved talking to my sister, she understood me so well. Every night she would listen to me blab on and on about my dates, without any judgement whatsoever. Our sisterhood was tight; we kept no secrets from one another.

"That's your third date this week—sounds serious," she said, peering over at me.

"Yeah, I really like him," I said, my voice swooning. "I guess I'll have to break it off with Derek."

Gwen laughed. "Your dating schedule is getting complicated. You're gonna have to start using a calendar."

"Ha ha . . . very funny."

"Well, at least you had fun. Okay, sis, I'm exhausted. Good night," she said, waving her hand.

"Good night, Gweny," I whispered.

This had become part of our nightly regiment—late night talks about my wild teen romances.

This is how it usually went: I would come home after curfew, climb up the trellis on the side of the house and enter my room through the bedroom window. Gwen, being the awesome sister that she was, would leave the latches unlocked and prop the window up about an inch so that I could open it. She also plumped up the pillow and bed sheets so that it looked like I was in bed on time—in case Mom or Dad came in to see us.

I'm not the bragging type but this was something we had perfected, regardless of the many dry runs we had in the beginning.

Gwen had fallen back asleep and was now snoring in her bed. A little too young to be riddled with something so disgusting, but who was I to judge. As her twin, I could end up with the same affliction merely for making fun of her. I had to be careful.

The house was quiet. Mom and Dad were asleep in the room across the hall. Adonis, our Siamese straggler was stretched out across my pillow. His paws dangled over my mouth as he lovingly blocked the air from my lungs.

His nightly ritual was to wander the house until the last bit of attention was sucked from each room. His last stop of the night always involved a romantic rendezvous with the hallway mirror for a final glimpse of his svelte physique. This was just my observation of course, I'm not too sure what he was doing. Because of this weird amorous relationship he had with his reflection, my parents were going to name him Narcissus. In the end they settled on Adonis. The name was fitting and he seemed to like it. After concluding his nightly affair with the mirror, he would saunter into my room and take reprieve among my pillow.

Our dog, Odin, was another story. Unlike Adonis, Odin was the protector of the house, caring more for others than himself. He was in short, the Army General. He rested nightly at the foot of Gwen's bed, keeping watch over the occasional shadow that crossed the floor. He was a monster of a German Shepherd—big enough to scare even Dad. And Dad never got scared. But Odin was a gentle giant. His biggest joy was to play with ladybugs. He never hurt them, he just liked to chase and herd them outside.

Kind of like the mailman . . . well sort of.

The mailman was a special case. He never came too close to our house. I guess he was a little nervous around Odin. I don't know why really, but every morning we would find our letters strewn across the front porch. And Odin *liked* this particular mailman. But whenever he went to say hello, the man would scream, drop his mail and dodge across the lawn like a chicken. Our sweet dog couldn't understand why the chicken didn't want to play. Poor Odin. He had a hard time making friends. He was a good guard dog though, and we were grateful for that.

I could hear his paws now, scraping the floor. He was most likely trying to capture a dust bunny, oh how they taunted him. His jaws opened and closed vigorously as he chomped on the air.

I looked over at the bed next to me and saw Gwen moving her lips by the glow of the moon. I laughed because she looked ridiculous. Looking out the bedroom window, I could see the moon beaming with light. And for whatever reason, I thought it was smiling.

My head was full of thoughts tonight and my nerves were keeping this body awake. I felt like someone was tugging on my eyelids. Slowly, I leaned my back against the wooden bed frame and sighed. Glancing over at the digital clock on the bedside table, I realized it was almost three o'clock in the morning. *Ouch, was I really out that late?*

And now I couldn't sleep. I guess I had a lot of things on my mind. Tomorrow, I had a geography exam and the day after that I had a physics final and I was worried that I hadn't studied enough for either of them. In all honesty, I thought my fifteenth year on this planet would be a little less stressful and a little more fun. No such luck. Gwen and I were going to be celebrating our sixteenth birthdays in a couple of weeks—at least that gave us something to look forward to.

Sixteen. Wow. We made it! To me that was a milestone. Maybe others wouldn't see it that way but they hadn't experienced what I had at such a young age. And it's what kept Gwen and I so close.

I was born with the name Samantha. My mom had a fascination with witches, and *Bewitched* was her favourite show. She was determined to name one of us that. My sister Gwen was born seven minutes before me: safe, sound and easy. But then I came out and all hell broke loose. Apparently, I was problematic for my mother. She reminded me of this practically every day especially when she was mad. I was troublesome, worrisome, painful and big. That was the first time anyone had ever heard her swear. And the first time she had ever pulled someone else's hair out—my dad's!

"She's not Samantha . . ." my dad would mockingly quote her words years after those horrendous hours of labour. "She's a demon!"

That comment would haunt me at the dinner table whenever the family needed a comedic moment. And whenever I broke curfew—which was often.

But with all due respect, that's not why my name was changed.

I was born Samantha. I became Scarlett.

Shortly after I was born, my fate was realized. I was born with a hole in my heart—a problem not even a joke could solve. This diagnosis rendered me vulnerable, not just physically but mentally as well. As I grew, my parents became more careful with me, restraining me from the daily activities of life. At first I liked it, being coddled by the arms that loved me. But then I started to wonder why I was being favoured.

"I know that you love me but what's wrong with Gweny?" I would ask. And of course my parents laughed at that.

My life was a busy one. It consisted of ongoing visits to the doctor's office, and various medications that became part of my daily diet. I was defiant from the beginning, refusing to take the pills. It forced my mom to be resourceful. She would break up the pills and put them in the jam, the peanut butter, or the milk. And that's when I caught her—I wondered what the white floating pieces were in my chocolate milk.

I knew something was different but everyone around me made me feel normal. Gwen had come to all the doctor's appointments with me, so I figured both of us were being examined. It really wasn't until I was eight that I realized my life was in fact, not the same as other kids'. I wasn't allowed to play any sports at school. Instead, I was forced into every non-athletic club my parents could think of.

One conversation I never forgot. "Mom—can I join the gymnastics team?" I asked one day at the kitchen table, holding the form tight in my excited little hands.

Well, you'd think I was asking for a tattoo or something. She turned to face me, hands covered in lemon-scented dish detergent and said, "Good Lord, Scarlett, why can't you just join the stamp club like normal kids?" I watched as the bubbles flew recklessly into the air as she swung her arms about, crazily. What an answer, I thought, but unfortunately not the one I wanted.

Other kids began to treat me differently at school. Some were nice. Some avoided me altogether, mostly because I wouldn't play sports with them. The thing that scared me the most was when Gwen started treating me differently—she was *too* nice. What I really wanted then, was an explanation. I knew the doctor's visits were for my heart but I realized that I hadn't been given all the information. My parents were hiding something from me.

One day, I learned what that was. It was the night they told me about the severity of my condition.

"Sit down," my father said to me one summer night. "Your mom and I need to tell you something."

"Scarlett—that's such a pretty name, don't you think?" my mother said.

I nodded. "I love my name. Why? What did I do this time?"

"You did nothing, sweetie," she smiled at me. "Now, do you know why we named you that?"

I didn't have an answer for her so I shook my head.

"Well, honey, it seemed fitting for you."

"But not Gweny?" I asked, innocently.

"Well, although you two are twins, you are different in certain ways. And you my dear have something that makes you very special." She paused, looked over at my father and then continued. "You know that scar that you have over your heart?" she pointed to my chest.

"Uh huh."

"It's something you've had since you were a baby. And it's time we told you how you got it."

She went on to explain the trials of surgery I experienced to correct this imperfection. And God bless her, never once did she describe my condition as a flaw or defect. This information was not meant to weaken me but rather waken me to the seriousness of my state of being. It was a smart move—informing me of my situation. Unfortunately, I didn't want to believe them.

The only part of the story I liked, was how my surgical scar was reflected in my name. And it's what eventually led me to accept my condition over time. This name was derived from inside of me. How cool was that! I found it empowering if anything.

Gwen had a scar too but the story behind hers wasn't nearly as exciting. She stopped the path of a soccer ball with her head one day at practise and ended up with a cut above her left eye. *My* scar and I had aged together but because she had to live with hers on her face, I had to cut her a little slack.

With time, I began to understand the compassion others showed me. Especially my sister. She was always there for me and I needed her a lot. We were the closest of sisters and I wouldn't have wanted it any other way.

Looking over at her now, I smiled. There she was—snoring away the night. On the floor laid our sergeant dog, licking the still air with his giant tongue. And perched now in front of the moonlit window, trying to catch a glimpse of his reflection, was our strange little feline.

What a weird family, I thought.

Little did I know, that it was about to get a whole lot weirder.

TO TELL TIME

"AND WHAT TIME did we tell you to come home?" My mother said, throwing the tea towel over her shoulder.

Reluctantly, I answered her, knowing very well where this line of questioning was headed. "Um, six o'clock?"

"That's right my dear. And what time is it now?"

Looking down at my watch, I cringed. "Nine o'clock."

"Honestly, Scarlett, did you think we wouldn't notice? It is *three* hours from when we told you to be home. And you missed dinner!"

"But on the bright side—I think I passed my physics and geography exams."

With emerald eyes, she glared at me. "Stop trying to change the subject."

"Mom, I was distracted at *school*—doesn't that count for something?"

"No, it doesn't. Not when the distraction is a boy."

"But he was really cute!"

"Oh? And what was this one's name?"

I shrugged. "I don't know—I didn't ask."

She looked at me, her arms crossed, her nose flaring. "This is inexcusable. This is the third time this week you've come home late for dinner, and might I add, the last time it's going to happen."

Geez, thank God she didn't know about my late night broken curfew. That would result in an all-out blown gasket. And I'd probably lose all window privileges as well.

"Tomorrow you're going to spend the entire day cleaning the attic," she said, with resolution.

My reaction must have been visible because my mother was pouncing on it before I even said a word. Boy was she fast.

"Scarlett—I don't want to hear it!"

"But tomorrow is Saturday! I have to spend the whole day cleaning the attic? The *whole* day?"

"Yes, my dear. The whole day," she said with a smile.

"But there's weird stuff up there—like Grandpa's long underwear and oil can collection."

"Oh, for Pete's sake, there's nothing up there that you wouldn't find in any other normal attic." She turned away and was now looking through the oven window at the meatloaf inside.

"This is like . . . child labour . . . . or something . . . cleaning the attic and all. What if I find a giant mouse or something while I'm up there?"

"Well, as long as it's not wearing Grandpa's long underwear," she laughed, "you should be fine."

"Very funny, Mom. Well can I at least take Adonis with me? Maybe he'll keep away any strange animals I find."

She laughed. "I doubt it, honey. He would probably just want their opinion on how he looked. But, yes you can take him. Just don't forget and leave him up there. He'd die if he went even two hours without looking in the mirror."

"How come Gweny doesn't have to do this?"

"Gwen does not have to clean the attic because *she* did not stay at school for three extra hours with a boy when *she* was supposed to be home." She opened the oven door. "Mmmm . . . doesn't that smell good? It's for tomorrow. That's your grandmother's meatloaf recipe—it's been passed down to all the women in the family and one day you'll have it too."

"Great, just great," I whimpered. "I have to clean the attic *and* eat meatloaf. Lucky me. Can I go to my room now?"

"We made you a plate of food from dinner—it's in the fridge. Why don't you eat that first."

I walked over to the fridge and opened the door. Sitting on a plate, staring back at me, was a collage of Brussels sprouts, carrots, and a pie of unknown origin. *Fantastic*, I thought. I grabbed the plate and the glass of milk that was standing beside it, closed the door and sadly made my way to the kitchen table. This meal was almost as unappetizing as the day I was about to spend up in the attic. I was not looking forward to either.

Tired and defeated, I tried to muster up the strength to down the plate of food in front of me. At least it was colourful—I'll give my mother that. She always said that 'Mixing foods with different colours was good for the spirit.' And boy did she try.

So there I was, nibbling away at the questionable food that lay before me as I sat silently and sulked. But then I had this weird feeling. It felt like something inside of me was telling me that I had to behave and do as I was told. And as much as I tried to sequester that part of me, I began to believe it.

I could hear my mother's voice now in the back of my head. "Frankly, Scarlett . . . I don't give a damn. You're going to clean the attic."

Great, just great.

DEAR DIARY

Diary Entry
Saturday July 6th, 2010

I'm in my room, getting ready for my day up in that dreaded attic. Oh good Lord above or mother Nature—whichever one of you is listening, could you do me just one little favour and rip the roof off of our house and take the attic with you? That way I wouldn't have to clean it and I'd have a great excuse. Actually, nevermind. Mom would know I was behind it and that we were in cahoots.

Okay, forget that last paragraph. I'm writing this because it might very well be my last entry. It is entirely possible that if I go into the attic—I may never return. I mean honestly, when was the last time anyone went up there? I think it was two years ago when Uncle Frankie went up to get a tennis racket but then he disappeared. Ooh . . . ahh. Okay, so he didn't really disappear. He was placed in the care of the Blue Meadow's nursing home staff but I won't get into that now. Let's just say that his trip to the home was finalized when he was decreed 'behaviourally unsound'—that was when Aunt Erma and Gwen found him chasing squirrels with a baseball bat. Good heavens.

Oh, Uncle Frankie, I miss you. If only we were able to talk to the animals like you did, then maybe we could understand why the gophers were trying to steal your lawn mower. Man, my family is crazy.

Well, I must push on. I will bring Adonis with me and together we will make our way to that wretched place. I will try to report back, but if I don't make it out alive—then Gweny can have all my stuff. Especially Frogger and Newton, my sweet little salamanders. Take care of them Gweny and feed them properly so that they don't eat each other.

Okay, no more stalling. I'm leaving my bedroom now.

Signing off,
Scarlett Cavanaugh

ATTIC UP!

S I POSITIONED the ladder under the ceiling door, I shuddered. I could see it now: a pair of ghostly arms reaching down to me, ripping me off of the floor as I disappear into the attic walls. My mind played out the scene over and over again. The only thing left behind would be my orange Converse sneakers—an indication to my family that I was indeed eaten by the attic people.

Boy, my imagination was creepy.

Still, I had that recurring thought: when *was* the last time anyone was up here? Mentally, I stapled the idea to my brain as I probed my mind for an answer. For the life of me, I couldn't come up with one. Someone must have been up here recently though.

Wait a minute, Dad was building something a couple months ago and he must have come up here for tools. The attic was where he kept everything. Our garage and basement were packed to the ceiling with all sorts of stuff, so he thought it would be easier to put his tools and hardware supplies in the attic. That was a comforting thought—Dad must have been up here. And *he* wasn't eaten by the attic people.

With that in mind, I climbed the silver steps, carefully placing my weight in the centre of them.

As I reached the top, I gently pushed the wooden opening to one side and poked my head up to look around. My first reaction was to sneeze.

"Holy bananas, it's dusty up here," I said, waving my hands in front of my face. "Whoa—it's dark too. I guess it would help if I turned the light on."

As I flipped the switch on the wall beside me, I realized that I was talking to myself. I looked below at the bottom of the ladder and saw Adonis gazing at his reflection in the metal.

"There you are, Mister. Come on—I'm not doing this alone." I stepped down the ladder and wrapped my arms tightly around his sleek body. Carefully, I climbed back up to the top and placed him on the dusty wooden floor. His initial reaction was the same as mine. He sneezed.

"I know—it's pretty dusty. Okay, wait right here, I'm going to open the window." I pulled myself up onto the floor and made my way over to the south-west side of the room. As I approached the window, I sighed. It was a grey kind of day. The overcast sky loomed with melancholy overtones. I unlocked the top of the glass and pushed it upwards, letting the fresh air permeate the room.

"Ahh . . . that's much better, don't you think bud?" I said, turning to face the cat.

He nodded his head in agreement.

"I swear, sometimes I think you know English."

Then I looked around at the surrounding space. And like an umbrella forced inside out by heavy winds, the smile I wore burst into a frown. *Holy cow!* There was so much stuff here. Although the attic was relatively large, it appeared smaller with everything that was stored inside of it. The task at hand now seemed slightly overwhelming.

"How could Mom possibly think I could clean all this in one day? It'll take more than that just to get through that stack of papers over there."

Adonis wasn't listening. Instead, he was making his way towards a pile of boxes that were stacked on top of each other in a corner. As he reached the boxes, he began to paw at a piece of burgundy velvet that was covering something behind them.

"What did you find, bud?" I said, walking towards him. "What is it? A secret hideaway? An old desk? Oh God, please don't say it's a mouse."

I watched his reaction as I removed the dark fabric. "Oh, for Pete's sake," I laughed. "I should have known."

Leaning against the wall was a large oval mirror surrounded by a deep chocolate mahogany frame.

"Wow . . . that looks pretty old. It sure is beautiful. I bet this was Grandma's." At the base of the mirror sat four large wooden feet, each carved into the shape of what looked like a lion's paw. "This is so cool."

Carefully, I brought the mirror up onto its feet. The frame was sturdy and sure-footed. It reminded me of some silly cartoon, where the mirror comes alive and runs around haphazardly as it tries to outwit the bedroom dresser that's chasing after it. That was a kooky thought.

I stood in front of the mirror and looked closely at the wood. "Whoever designed this must have taken their time—there's so much detail to it." Slowly, I traced the pattern of wood with my fingers. "Mom never told me about this." I then knelt down to look at the feet.

Adonis sat next to me, purring as he watched my hands move along the curvature of the frame. I looked over at him and noticed that he was now staring at my eyes. I felt something stir in the fresh air that surrounded me, a strange awakening or something. "Do you really understand me?"

Of course he said nothing. He just meowed and turned his head to gaze into the mirror. I shook my head. "I'm too young to go crazy. Sorry Uncle Frankie—I'm not ready to join you at the home yet."

I stood, brushed the dust off of my knees and scanned the room. There were so many things up in this attic. Dad's tools, Mom's quilting and knitting items, Grandma and Grandpa's household appliances, Gweny's and my baby stuff. I felt a momentary sigh of relief when I saw only board games in one corner—at least those would be easy to sort.

"Well, I guess I have to start somewhere." I took the velvet fabric and spread it across the floor so as to bring some comfort to my sitting area. I then knelt down in front of the mirror and began to open, one by one, the boxes that were stacked before me.

*　　*　　*

After sorting through many of the boxes, my fingers were starting to get tired. "Oh Adonis, this is so boring. These boxes are all filled with bills and receipts. There's nothing even remotely interesting here." Peering over at the cat, I realized that he had fallen asleep belly up with his legs in the air. He looked so funny.

Just then, I heard someone climbing the ladder. My father poked his head up. "Hey kiddo—how about some lunch? I made you an egg sandwich and a salad."

"Oh, thanks. There's just one more box I want to sort through—then I'll be down. I think I'm on a roll here."

"That's great. How's it going up here?"

"Well, I opened the window because it was so dusty. Oh, and look what I found," I said, pointing to the mirror beside me. "Was this Grandma's mirror?"

"Hmm . . . I think it was your grandmother's but I can't say for sure. You'd have to ask your mom. Listen, I've got to go wash some mud off my boots, they got pretty dirty on my walk through Blue Beacon. And you know how I hate dirt," he smiled.

I laughed internally. My father was such a clean freak. Yet, most of his extra-curricular time was spent outdoors either hiking or climbing.

"You and I should go sometime, kiddo."

"I don't know, I think you should take Mom." I was too old to go on walks with my parents. Besides, that was the place I usually went to with my dates, or when I just wanted to be alone with the moon and think about life.

"Well, when you're through with that box, be sure to come down for something to eat."

"Will do, Dad."

He took one final glimpse of the attic and smiled. "Wow—this place looks better already."

"Dad—I haven't moved anything yet."

"Oh . . . well . . . it still looks good. Okay, I'll leave your lunch on the kitchen table." With that, he climbed down the ladder and walked away.

Sitting in front of me was the last box in the pile. Picking it up, I noticed some strange markings on the lid. They looked like a code of some sort, scribbled in someone's hand-writing. "Finally—something interesting."

Personally, I loved putting secret codes on things and it was something I appreciated in others. Codes were wicked. They were challenging and fun to figure out. Gwen and I had invented our own secret code when we were young. But as I advanced in the department, she outgrew it. So I kept my secret language to myself—I was the only one who could read it.

I tried to make out the markings on the box. For a moment I pondered the letters. And then it hit me. I knew what it said. Written on the lid were four words, *For Our Eyes Only*. I flipped the box over but saw nothing else on it. "Hmm, that's interesting. Gweny must have written that." Part of me doubted that though, she didn't know how to use the code anymore.

The box was sealed, with red ribbon holding the lid tightly in place. I tried to unknot the ribbon but that was a failed attempt. I sat for a few minutes trying to pry open the box, hoping to rip the cardboard around the ribbon but that didn't work either. The cardboard was like steel.

I jumped to my feet when I heard the words "Use the scissors," cut through the air from somewhere behind me.

"Who said that?" I yelled.

No answer.

I waited for a reply. Looking around the room, I squinted. "Okay—look, I know what I heard and I refuse to believe that it was just my imagination."

Still, no answer.

Then I saw something shiny over by my old Malibu Barbie station wagon. On the floor beside the toy, were two knitting needles and a pair of pocket scissors.

As I walked over to pick them up, I heard a noise behind me. I grabbed the nearest thing and turned around quickly.

Sitting by the box, now playing with the ribbon, was Adonis.

When I realized just how ridiculous I looked, holding a pair of knitting needles protectively in front of me, I sighed. "Adonis—you scared me. I don't know why, I guess this room just gives me the creeps."

I placed the needles back on the floor and grabbed the scissors. Walking back to the box, I directed the cat towards another corner and sat back down. I took the scissors and cut the ribbon from around the lid.

Oddly enough, the lid came off with ease as I set it to one side. Inside the box was an object surrounded by crimson tissue. As I lifted the tissue, a small book was revealed. *Jackpot!* Finally—something juicy I could sink my teeth into. As I pulled out the book, I realized what it was: a diary.

"Wait a minute, this looks just like *my* diary from downstairs. Great—I thought mine was one of a kind, a special birthday gift from Mom and Dad. Who does this belong to?"

Up until three years ago, all of Gwen's and my gifts had come in twos. This was the first time our parents had broken tradition. For our thirteenth birthdays, Gwen got a bag of polished stones and I got a hand-crafted diary pressed with real roses.

Then my train of thought jumped tracks. This diary looked like it had been used. The colour was slightly drained from the original pink cover, and the book was thick and propped up—a sign that something was most likely written inside of it. But if it was anything like the one I had downstairs, then it would have a key.

Turning it over, I looked for the key to open it. As I flipped it right side up I realized that there was no need for a key—the book was unlocked.

"That's weird. I *always* lock mine. I guess whoever owned this didn't want to use the key."

Although there was something oddly familiar about this diary, much of it seemed new. I thought about how it could be familiar to me but there was just no way. I had never seen this book before. *My* diary was hidden in my room—its location known only to Gwen.

Maybe this was one of those times when Mom spoke about getting déjà vu and amnesia at the same time.

I shrugged it off.

Gently, I opened the cover as my eyes began skimming the words. They stopped when I reached the bottom of the page. Slowly, the book dropped from my hands as it sank to the floor.

Staring up at me from the printed page was my name, in my hand writing. Clear as day, it said Scarlett Cavanaugh.

And the year was 2012.

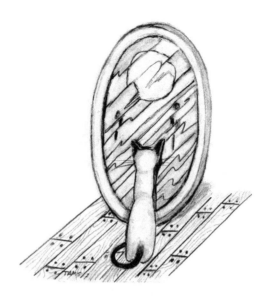

FAMILIAR

I DIDN'T WANT to touch it. I just sat there, gazing down at the book, hoping that it was just my imagination.

Thoughts raced through my mind. The first was that Uncle Frankie was behind this—his last hurrah before he went to the nursing home. He used to love pulling pranks on the family. But that was two years ago already, it couldn't have been him. Then I thought maybe it was Gwen, perhaps this was a trick she was playing on me. But then I tossed that idea away. It was too detailed, too devilishly elaborate to be Gwen. Besides, she had better things to do with her time than freak me out. That just wasn't her style.

I sat silently on the burgundy velvet fabric with my hands neatly tucked into my lap. The fabric was now my lifeboat and I could see the attic floor moving up and down with small hungry sharks hiding in amongst the wooden waves. My imagination was taking over again and I felt that if I just stayed still, then the rational part of my mind would eventually put me at ease.

Closing my eyes, I breathed in deeply. In and out. In through the nose, out through the mouth. I felt my heart begin to calm. Maybe Mom and

Dad were behind this trick. Yeah—those crazy parents of mine. And this was my punishment, to clean the attic. Of course! It had to be them.

"Maybe it was Professor Plum . . . in the library . . . with a candlestick," I heard a man's voice behind me.

My eyes popped open as I spun around on my knees. "Dad? Is that you?" I looked around the area where the voice came from but saw only boxes and dust.

"Or perhaps it was Colonel Mustard in the dining room with the wrench," a voice came from the other side of the attic.

I had never jumped to my feet so fast, not even when I saw that brown recluse spider crawling on my bed a few years ago. "Who's there?" I called out.

There was no answer. My eyes desperately searched the room, hoping to find the source of the words. "Look—I know I heard something. Who's there?"

"I'll give you a clue . . ." a whisper came from behind me. As I turned to look, the only thing I saw was my own reflection in the mahogany-framed mirror. A momentary twinge rolled up my spine when I thought I saw someone else looking back at me. My goose bumps descended slightly when I realized it was only me, although admittedly they were still the size of mountains.

My ears perked when I heard the wood creaking ever so softly in the corner behind me. I looked into the mirror to see if I could spot this verbal intruder. "I know you're there . . . whoever you are. And I don't know what you want but if you don't reveal yourself then I'm gonna scream and call for my dad. Then you'll really be in trouble. Yeah, that's right. He's big and he loves his baseball bat and would destroy anything that hurt his daughter. GOT IT?!"

"You need another clue?" a soft voice came from around me.

"Is this some kind of game—trying to make me go nuts like Uncle Frankie? Because it's not gonna work buddy. I'm as sane as the next person. Well . . . mostly."

There was no answer.

"Fine—give me another clue."

"Ahh—now you're catching on."

"Catching on to what?" I asked, looking around the room. I was determined to keep my heart from blowing right out of my chest.

"Perhaps it was Miss Scarlett . . . in the attic . . . with her mind."

Uh oh, I thought. *He knows my name. A momentary setback. Come on Scarlett . . . don't be afraid. Be strong.* "How do you know my name?" I said, trying not to show any emotion.

"Oh I know a lot of things."

Now I felt like I was being surrounded—by my own questions nonetheless. "Look buddy—I'm about to grab those knitting needles over there and I'm warning you—I'm not afraid to use them."

"What knitting needles?"

As I looked back at the floor, I noticed that the needles were gone. *Why that crafty little . . .* "Fine! I don't actually need knitting needles to protect me. I know karate. Deal with that, Mister!"

"You don't know karate. Nice try though."

"How do you know that?" I asked, my body standing still in place.

"I know a lot about you, Scarlett. More than you know about yourself."

"That's impossible—how could someone I've never seen before, know anything about me?"

"Oh—we've known each other for a long time, my dear. You just don't recognize me."

"What are you talking about? I can't even see you. And if you know me so well, then you should know better than to scare me. I have a heart condition."

"You're not scared."

"Oh—I'm not? That's interesting because I think I am."

"No . . . you're not. You were startled at first. But now you want to play my game."

"I'm too old for games . . . whoever you are."

"I don't think so. Look at those board games in the corner. You knew it would be the easiest part of the attic to clean."

"Wait a minute . . . how did you know that? I never said that out loud. I just thought it."

"I know. I heard."

"You heard my thoughts?"

"Yes."

Good grief. I wonder if he can hear what I'm thinking right now?

"I can."

Cripes. "Okay, who are you?" Now more than ever I wanted to know who the voice belonged to.

"Look behind and you will see . . . something you know but won't believe."

Slowly I turned. There, stacked in a tall pile, were five or six coloured boxes. On top of them, sitting upright and looking back at me, was my cat.

"Adonis—there you are. Where've you been buddy?" My eyes continued searching for the voice but soon stopped when the answer I was waiting for, came in the most unexpected form.

"I've been here the whole time—with you."

My body straightened. The hairs on the back of my neck and arms straightened too. I was now stiff as a board. I looked over at Adonis and gasped. "Oh good heavens . . . I'm going crazy. It's finally happened. I think my cat is talking to me."

"Of course I'm talking to you, silly. Who else would I be talking to? You're the only one here."

I could feel my eyelids widen as my nervous system kicked in to high gear. "Oh my God!"

"Well thank you," he said, "but that's not my name."

"Are . . . you smiling?" I asked, my head trying to rationalize this obscure event.

"Yes, yes I am."

My words felt crooked and sporadic as they left my lips. "Cats . . . can't . . . talk . . . can they?"

"Why not? I like to talk."

I just looked at him sitting there all high and mighty on his delusional throne of cardboard. Apparently, I had lost my marbles. And also I was staring.

"Didn't your parents tell you that it's not nice to stare?"

"I'm sorry . . . it's just that . . . you're talking . . . to *me*."

"I thought we went over that already."

"Yeah, but I've never talked to you before. I've never talked to *any* cat before."

"Well, I'm just glad that you were finally ready to listen. Before today, you weren't ready for me."

I couldn't take my eyes off of his little whiskered mouth. "I mean . . . your lips . . . are moving," I pointed at his face.

"Boy, you're having a really hard time with this, aren't you? And stop pointing. Didn't your parents teach you *any* manners?"

I nodded.

"Maybe it would help if I introduced myself."

I interjected. "Wait . . . we've already met. You're Adonis—our cat."

"Well, as flattered as I am with that name—and don't get me wrong I do love it—it's not actually my name."

"It's not?"

"No, it's not. My name is Habock."

I said nothing. I mean, what was I supposed to say? I had no idea. And for once I was speechless. My tongue was tied. All I could do was watch this fictitious scene play out before me.

"I'm not fictitious."

"How do you know? I've had some crazy imaginative ideas, stories, dreams—you name it. How do I know for sure that you're not one of them? Maybe I'm sleeping right now."

"You're not sleeping." With that, he raised his paw and blew a brown sparkly substance into my face.

I raised my head and let out a giant sneeze. "What did you do that for?" I said, lifting my sleeve to my nose.

"I just wanted to show that you were in fact, awake," he smiled. "If you like I could scratch you with my claw."

"No, no, that won't be necessary," I said, stepping back from him. "So your name isn't Adonis?"

"No. It's Habock. And it's good to finally talk to you, Scarlett."

I felt ridiculous saying the words out loud but who else would know? "It's good to talk to you too, Habock. I'm sorry, this is just all so weird."

"So? You've seen weird before."

"Not this weird. Can I ask you a question? Why now—why here in the attic?"

"Well, I needed you up here because we have much to talk about. That, and you have something that belongs to me," he said, pointing his paw towards the mirror.

"That's *yours?*"

"Yes, it belongs to my family."

"You have family? Where are they?" I said, looking around.

"Scarlett, my family is through that mirror—they're waiting for me on the other side. I'm the only one who came here—to this time. I came to find you because we need your help."

"You need *my* help? What on Earth for? And why today? You've been with us since I was a baby."

"Well, to be honest, we needed you to grow up. For that, I had to watch over you. And that took time. We were willing to wait until you were ready."

"Um . . . ready for what, exactly?" I still couldn't believe I was having a conscious articulate conversation with my cat. But it was starting to grow on me.

"You'll soon find out. But it's time for me to go back now. And for that, I need your help. The powers that be have been very busy lately preparing for you. And the time has come for you to take control of the future. It lies in your hands, Scarlett—whether you wish to believe it or not."

"I don't understand. You mean *my* future?"

"Not just yours . . . all of ours," he said, jumping down from the boxes. He spoke as he walked over to the mirror. "This isn't just any mirror, Scarlett. It's the future. And the time has come for you to see it."

ACCEPTING WHAT'S NEW

"SO, YOU'RE TELLING me that if I walk through this mirror, then I'll be in the future?"

"Yes." Habock then turned and walked over to the diary on the floor. "It's not a lie, Scarlett, and it's not your imagination. This diary is yours from the future—two-and-a-half years in the future."

I stepped away from the mirror and knelt down beside the book. Picking it up, I shook my head. "You mean this really is my diary? This is *my* writing?"

"Yes. Things change in the next few years of your life. You decide to hide it up here—safe from dangerous eyes."

"Dangerous eyes? What is that . . . code for something? Cause I like codes."

"No, it's no code. There are beings in your future that are after this book."

"Well if that's the case, then why didn't I lock it?"

"You didn't need to—you felt that it wouldn't be found. In fact you left it unlocked because there was only one person that your future self trusted to find it," he said looking up at me.

"Oh, and who was that?"

"You, Scarlett."

I stood with the book in my hands and began to pace back and forth. "Adonis . . . I mean Habock . . . how do you know all of this if you've been with me all this time?"

"Because I came from the future. I arrived in the past when you were just a baby. I waited until now to reveal myself, right before you turn sixteen. You see, this is when your life starts to change."

"That's in a few weeks. Gweny and I are having a big party with all of our friends."

"I know. The night of your party is when things get derailed."

I stopped to look down at him. "What are you talking about?"

"Scarlett, there's someone waiting for you in the future, waiting for the moment you're alone so that they can turn you. It happens the night of your party."

"*Turn* me? What am I, a war criminal? I don't know anybody like that."

"I know . . . but I do. It's why I waited all this time and it's why we have to act right now," he said.

"Well, who is it?" I searched his eyes for an answer.

His response was vague. "Someone, you'll soon find out."

"Great, you're just as cryptic as my parents."

Habock just stared at me. He had this strange look that I had never seen before in a cat. It was almost human. He acted like a person, with expressions only exhibited by the movement of human facial muscles. I wanted to pick him up and cuddle him like a baby—

"Scarlett, you're drifting off . . . Scarlett . . . pay attention! I know I'm cute but we're not going to have any of this baby business!"

I shook my head as his words brought me back to where I was standing. "I'm sorry—it's just that you're so cute and cuddly."

"Well, thank you. But we have to focus here." He began to pace in front of the mirror.

"Wait a minute. How did you know I would be sent to the attic today? You couldn't possibly have known that. That was Mom's idea. And what about that boy from school—he's the reason I'm up here."

"Let's just say that I have a couple tricks up my sleeve. The boy at school was my idea. He wanted to talk to you anyway. I just gave him a shove."

"Are you serious?"

Habock laughed. "I *can* talk you know. A little sight, unseen. Besides, I felt like he would be good for you and someone that might also help us. And as for your mom's idea—well, hardly. I used a telephone and pretended I was your dad calling from elsewhere. I simply suggested that your punishment be to clean the attic."

"You were behind all of this? That's incredible. Wait—is that why my phone bill was so steep this month?"

"Scarlett . . . focus!"

"Sorry," I said with a sheepish grin.

"Well, I can't take all the credit for that boy you know. You did take the bait—which is precisely my point here. You are your own person and I understand that. But this is the time in your life when you tend to be influenced by others—you're highly impressionable right now. It's the whole fitting in 'teen thing'—I get it. But I want to change that."

I crossed my arms and looked down my nose at him. "I am *not* influenced! I have a mind of my own you know."

"Oh, don't get me wrong, I know that you're in control of yourself. You're also stubborn, defiant, bull-headed, and undeniably insolent when it comes to . . ."

"Okay, okay, I get the picture . . . but what?"

"But that's what's going to get you into trouble," he said.

"Why should I believe that? Why should I believe any of this?"

"Because it's the truth—it's what happens in time."

"So what if I choose not to believe you—what then?"

His turquoise eyes stared up at me and for a moment my heart melted just looking at him. "Scarlett, I would never hurt you. Please believe me. We need your help to change what is coming."

"But how do I know who to trust, and how will I know what to do?" I could feel his emotions penetrating through my tough hide.

"I will help you," he said.

We were momentarily interrupted when I heard someone climbing the ladder. I turned and saw my father placing a plate of food and a folded napkin on the attic floor. "Okay kid, here's some lunch. You didn't come down, and your mom and I got a little worried. You've been up here for a while now." He looked around the room and then smiled at the floor. "How's Adonis doing up here—I see he's a big help."

When I looked down, I couldn't help but roll my eyes. Habock had fallen asleep on my shoes. "Yeah—he's a real impediment," I laughed.

"Okay Scarlett, your mom and I are going out for a while this afternoon, and Gwen's at soccer practice until eight o'clock tonight. So you've got the house to yourself. We'll lock the doors when we leave so you can stay up here as long as you need to."

He must have realized that something in me had changed. "Are you okay? You seem different somehow."

"I'm fine, Dad," I said, gazing over at the mirror. "I guess I just needed a little time to figure things out. I'll see you later tonight."

"Okay, see you kid." With that he left.

A moment later, Habock's eyes opened. "It's good that they're leaving," he said, stretching out his paws.

"Geez, are you narcoleptic or something? You seem to fall asleep really easily."

"I'm a *cat*," he scoffed. "What else am I supposed to do with my time?"

I shook my head, embarrassed. "I walked right into that one, didn't I? Okay, so why is it good that they're leaving?"

Habock spoke as he wandered towards the mirror. "Because this afternoon will be a learning experience for you and it's better that you do it alone. In an empty house."

Looking around the attic, I thought about my past. My childhood toys and board games were in one corner while some of my parent's things were in another. Over by the window was a box of Uncle Frankie's clothing and lying next to it were several storage bins containing my grandparent's belongings.

My life was here and I didn't want that to change. Now, I was presented with problems from the future. I had no idea what awaited me there, but I began to believe that whatever was happening right now was happening for a reason. Reality or not, I guess I needed to believe Habock. All I hoped was that he knew what he was doing. And that I would remember every detail when the men in white jackets came to take me away to the funny farm.

TO ANOTHER PLACE

 SAT NOW by the empty plate, wiping my mouth with the napkin. "Oh, that was good. Dad was right—I needed that."

"I bet it's not as good as Quarsfin . . ." Habock said.

The name alone made me squeamish. "I don't even want to know what that is."

"It's a delicious type of bluefish. Scientists haven't found it yet but they will in about two years."

"Really? That's kind of cool, actually . . ." I said, drifting off.

"Okay, Scarlett, I don't mean to be a nag but it's time we got on with things."

"Wait a minute, you really want me to drop everything and go right *now?*" I stood up and walked over to him. "What about Odin? I can't just leave him here alone."

"You're kidding right? That dog can take care of himself. Trust me, I know." Habock sat on his haunches, pointing to the window. "Go look for yourself."

I marched across the floor. As I reached the window, I saw the giant Oak tree in the backyard and the red doghouse shaped like a fire station sitting underneath it. I gazed around the yard but couldn't see Odin, so I called for him. "Odin—where are you big guy? Odinnn . . ." I beckoned.

Out from the corner of the yard, he ran. He heard my voice and looked up at me.

"Hey there buddy . . . you okay down there?" I said, leaning out the window.

He acknowledged my words with a bark. Then a squirrel ran along the top of the fence beside him and he was off in pursuit.

Turning back, I giggled. Odin was such a sweet dog. God bless who ever came between him and the neighbourhood squirrels.

"I was right, wasn't I?" Habock smiled at me.

"Yes, you were right—he's fine," I conceded.

"Dogs are such funny creatures. Plus yours seems to have an attention deficit disorder. He's very hard to talk to . . . you know from one animal to another. I'd be asking him how his day was and there he'd go, leaving me for a rubber toy."

"Yeah . . . right," I laughed. "You're one to talk. 'Oh—look how beautiful I look in the mirror. I just can't get enough of myself . . . I'm so handsome'," I mocked him. "Geez—you're worse than any teenage girl I know."

"Actually—that's not quite what I was doing," he said, walking over to the window. "Although it does explain the name you gave me. What I was trying to do was communicate with my family using the other mirrors in the house, since I couldn't get to this one without someone opening the attic door."

"Oh . . . sorry. I just thought you were being vain."

"It's okay," he said. He then jumped onto the windowsill. "Look at that. Do you see the moon?"

I leaned out the window again and looked up at the sky. The clouds had broken, revealing the blue buoyant sea behind them. Perched above the land, was the big round moon. "Yeah—there it is. What about it?"

"Well, the moon is very important in the future. We have a special name for it."

"The future? You mean the one that's two-and-a-half years ahead of this one? You've *named* the moon?"

"Yes, two-and-a-half years from now things have changed—many of these changes have to do with the moon. It's been given the name *Avari*."

"That's a pretty name. Why is it called that?"

"You'll soon find out. In fact when we go to the future, you can ask it."

I leaned back in and stared at Habock. "Pardon me, did you just say I could *ask the moon*? What—is it alive or something?"

"Or something," was all he said.

"Habock, that doesn't even make any sense. The moon *has* no light—it's just light reflected from the sun."

"Yes, that is the logical answer . . . but it's not the right one. Avari's light comes from within. She is very much alive, which is why we can talk to her."

"Oh, of course. How stupid of me," I joked.

Habock smiled. "Scarlett, I have so much to teach you. You have an imaginative mind. Surely you can be open to something like this."

I nodded. "Okay, sure . . . I'll be open. I mean, why wouldn't I want to talk to the moon? I'm talking to my cat right now." Then I paused. "Hey, why don't I just ask 'the Man in the Moon'—he must have all the answers. Maybe he can tell me what kind of cheese it's made out of!"

"Okay now you're just being ridiculous," he shook his head at me. "There's no such thing as 'the Man in the Moon' and how on Earth did we get on the topic of cheese? Good God, what have they been teaching you in school?"

I just stared at him, blankly.

With a careful leap, he jumped onto the floor and made his way back to the mirror. "Come now Scarlett, there is much to be done. Time is of the essence."

Hesitantly, I walked back to where he was standing. "I just don't know. This is really strange."

He watched me for a moment and then rubbed his chin with his paw.

I had to remind myself that this was in fact, a cat.

"Tell you what . . . if you do this for me, then I'll help you with your parents."

"What do you mean?" I was curious about where his thoughts were headed.

"What if I were able to help you out with one of your boyfriends? Perhaps I could give your parents a nudge and make them a little more receptive towards a particular situation."

"What situation? You mean, so that I could bring a boyfriend home, or that my parents would have more trust in me?"

"Both," he smiled.

"You could do that?"

"Absolutely, if you just come with me now."

I thought about his proposal. "Okay—I'll do it." I stretched out my hand towards him. "Let's shake on it."

Habock reached out his paw and together we shook. "Good. Now let's get moving," he said.

I looked over at the mirror. "So, you want me to step through this mirror . . . into the future . . . with you."

"Yes."

"And once I get there, will I see my future self or my family?"

"You might see them but I can't let you meet them, Scarlett. You'll have to stay hidden—it could affect what happens in their future as well."

"Are you saying that I get to go to the future but I can't come into contact with my own family?"

"It's for the best, trust me. I'll explain more when we get there. We should probably go together. Pick me up and hold on to me. Then put one foot in front of the other. You'll feel the way."

I looked down at him and sighed. "Okay, but listen, if I end up wearing a straight jacket because of this—then I'm taking you with me. This is so crazy. I can't believe that I'm actually doing this."

I reached down and picked him up. "You know, I'm always surprised at how light you are, considering how much you eat. You're as light as a feather."

"Don't talk about feathers," he grimaced. "I'm really hungry right now. We have work to do, so let's focus!"

"Okay—here we go!" Holding Habock tight in my arms, I took my first step into the unknown. I could feel the mirror melt as I placed my left foot in front of it. It felt soft as it wrapped itself around my ankle. "This feels weird."

"It's alright, Scarlett. Just hold on to me and keep on stepping."

I watched as the mirror moulded itself around my leg. It felt inviting as it reeled the rest of my body into the material.

Although I could feel part of me holding back, the other part was letting go and getting stronger. My excitement mounted as the shiny material moved its way up my body. Whatever hesitations I had, were disappearing. My fears were being released. As the rest of my body moved through the frame, I felt a calm wash over me, as if I were drifting in a sea of tranquil waters. Gently I moved through space and time as darkness took my sight.

Then suddenly, a flash of bright light sparked my senses to life as I heard my name being called out. Opening my eyes, I gasped.

To my surprise, I knew exactly where I was. And oh what a joy it was to see it.

UNSEEN, UNHEARD

ABOCK—IT'S THE ATTIC! Oh thank God, I thought we were gonna end up somewhere weird. What a relief," I sighed.

"Well, not quite," he said, jumping down to the floor.

I watched as he searched the room for something. "What are you looking for?"

He didn't answer. With cautious steps, he made his way to the attic door and then walked over to the window. "Everything seems normal—mind you, I haven't been here for a little while. The unfortunate part is that the attic door is closed—we can't open it from up here. We might have to climb out the window to get to where we're going."

"Are you serious? I'm not climbing out there. Do you know how high up we are?"

"What's the difference—you climb up to your bedroom window practically every night."

"Yeah, but this is higher," I said, smugly.

"Scarlett, now is not the time to be scared."

"Well, can't you use your influence to make someone open the attic door like you did with my family?"

"This *is* your family. It's just a few years in the future—don't forget that."

"Right, sorry."

At that moment I heard a voice calling my name below. "Scarlett—the phone's for you." It sounded like my mother.

"Remember," Habock said, "we have to be very careful not to be seen. That's your mother calling for you. The *future* you."

I nodded in response as I tried to listen to the voice below. Although the walls were thin, what I heard was barely audible. I had to get lower to the floor to hear. As I bent down, my knee hit the wood—hard. I was surprised at how the sound carried through the room.

Habock quietly walked up alongside me and shook his head in disgust. "What did I say about not being seen? And let's not forget about being heard, too," he whispered.

He had that look of disappointment down pat—I felt like I was being reprimanded by a teacher or parent. Maybe that look was universal in the cat world too.

"Sorry—didn't mean to," I shrugged.

As I shook off my feline disciplinarian, I listened again to the voice below. With my ear to the floor, I waited for a response to my mother's call.

Then I heard something.

"Habock," I mouthed, "I think it's coming from my room downstairs." Quiet as a mouse this time, I crawled across the floor in the direction of my bedroom, assuming that it was still mine in the future. I then laid my head on the dusty floor and listened to the conversation below. "I think she . . . I mean me . . . is in my room," I said, peering over at him.

He nodded in response.

"Okay, Sparks," I heard from beneath me, "I'll meet you tonight. Bring what you have. I'll tell my mom that I'm going over to Julie's house."

Footsteps moved through the downstairs hallway as the bedroom door opened and another voice entered the room.

"Scarlett, what are you doing?" the other voice said.

"Oh, for Pete's sake, Gwen—ride another horse. This one's tired of you beating it!"

"Don't be so dramatic, Scar. You know Mom wants you home tonight."

"It's none of your business, Gwen. Butt out or I'll kick your butt!"

I gasped. Not just at the words but at the nasty, sneering tone my future self was using—and to Gweny!

"It *is* my business when I'm supposed to be the one using the car tonight," Gwen said. "I have plans and they don't include you. Plus, you've got homework to do."

"What are you—my babysitter? Just leave me alone."

I heard a scuffle below and then a loud smack. The conversation continued.

"That was my friend, Gwen. You had no right to hang up on him!"

"Let me guess, that friend's name is Sparks? You know you're not supposed to talk to him. He's a bad influence."

"I don't care what you think."

"Scar, I'm just trying to help."

"Gwen—I don't need your help. In fact, I don't need you at all. I wish you'd just disappear!"

Oh my God—what was I saying? Disappear? *Disappear?* That couldn't be me! I would never talk that way to my sister. I was utterly stunned at what I was hearing but still I continued to listen.

"Why are you so mad at me, Scar? You never used to treat me like this."

"Go away, Gwen. I don't want to talk to you. Just leave me alone."

With that, I heard the bedroom door slam and what I could only think of as weeping on the other side of it.

Slowly, I sat up and looked around the attic. Habock was sitting by the window staring up at the sky.

As I got to my feet, I thought about the conversation I had just heard. "That can't be me. I would never treat Gweny like that. Never. Not even in a million years."

Habock jumped off of the windowsill and made his way over to where I was standing. His voice low, he explained the situation to me. "It *is* you, Scarlett. This is what I wanted to show you. You *have* changed."

"But that can't be me! I mean . . . look at me. This is me, standing here right now. *This,* is who I really am."

"Not in the future. Which brings me back to what I said before. The influence others have on you is very powerful."

"Okay—who are you talking about? I want to know. Please tell me."

"Very well, Scarlett. They are called the Mirrorwalkers and they are very dangerous."

"Who are they?"

"They are the ones who are about to change your future, in the past that is—the one we just came from. They sent in one of their own to recruit you the night of your sixteenth birthday party. They are a fearless band of nocturnal creatures and they are out to change the future of the world."

"Why?" I asked.

"For their own domination, of course. But the Mirrorwalkers believe that *you* are the key to changing it. That's why they're after you."

"Well, can't you just explain to them that they've got the wrong person and that I don't have what they're looking for? It's as simple as that, right?"

He looked up at me with tender eyes. "If it were as simple as that then I wouldn't have brought you here. The problem runs deeper. Once the Mirrorwalkers recruit you, you become a force of darkness. You escape their wrath but only temporarily. Once they summon you back—that's it, you're finished. You become one of them."

"I can't believe I would ever do that," I said, doubting his words.

"Sadly, you do. It's okay though because I had a plan of my own. That's why we've come here today—to see the future and to find out whether my plan has worked. I wanted to know how you turned out. You see, the Mirrorwalkers picked you, Scarlett, knowing very well that you would turn. I knew otherwise."

My eyes bounced all over the room like a rogue missile off course. I couldn't believe that I would ever do something so extreme as to join a band of dark dwellers, or that I would fall so easily into their hands. "There's no way I would've gone willingly."

"I know that, more than anyone. I know what lies inside of you. Think of your scar and what lies beneath it. It's your heart," he smiled up at me. "And trust me—it's *not* weak."

Placing my hand over my chest, I gasped. "My heart? They're after my *heart?*"

"In a way, yes. The Mirrorwalkers believe that the hole in your heart is your greatest weakness and to a degree it is. But it's also what makes you strong. You are a paradox within yourself. And that's why this problem cannot be solved with a simple explanation."

"How did they get so strong?"

Habock gave me a look of concern, like what he was about to say would admit defeat by simply saying it. "Kingdoms were overthrown. It all started with the mighty Seeing stones."

"What are those?"

"Those are the stones that protected three powerful Kingdoms: the Batfish, the Sparrowhawks and the Cats. These large, black mountain stones were placed around the Kingdom's walls so that those living within them could detect evil that approached. But once the stones fell into the hands of evil, the walls were breached and the Kingdoms were taken. As were all their powers."

"What kind of powers are we talking about here?" The concept sounded completely foreign but still part of me wanted to hear the story.

"The kind that destroys goodness, once it's in the hands of evil. The stones can harness the power over water, land and air."

"Wow . . . that pretty much covers everything. These stones, where are they now?"

"They lie in the hands of the Mirrorwalkers."

"That's not good, is it?"

"No—it's not. We are going to change that, though. I promise. First we have to . . ." he stopped.

"We have to what?" I asked.

"Sshhh . . . I heard something." Habock's ears perked as he moved towards the attic door.

I heard it too—footsteps climbing a ladder, heading for the attic.

"Someone's coming," he whispered. "Quick—cover the mirror."

With silent steps, I crept across the wooden floor towards the mirror. I found the dark fabric that was also present in this time and threw it over the frame.

I looked over at Habock and saw him crouched in a corner behind some large boxes.

"Scarlett, come here. Hide!" he motioned to me.

As noiseless as I could, I made my way over to where he was hiding and knelt down. We both watched as the attic door slowly lifted off of the floor and slid to one side. Then, a young woman dressed all in black, raised herself up into the room.

"Oh my God!" I whispered.

She immediately stood and made her way towards a pile of boxes by the window. I couldn't believe what I was seeing. I looked over at Habock with a shocked expression. His paw was placed over his mouth—he was signalling me to remain still and quiet.

Gazing back at the scene that played out before me, I shook my head in disbelief.

Never, had I ever expected to see this.

MIRROR IMAGE

OGETHER, WE WATCHED as a young woman with my face, sat on the floor sorting through various items. We remained quiet behind the boxes, hoping that our presence would go undetected.

All I could think of was her profile. She was wearing my face. It felt so creepy. How could both of us have the same face?

She didn't look much different after two years of aging. Her hair was the same—brown and straight, shoulder length with bangs. She was make-up-less, and slightly paler than me. The only real difference was the lip glimmer that I wore religiously and carried with me every day. She clearly didn't have any on. But when I looked at her eyes, I saw inside of her. A glassy frost shone through her hazel depression. It was like looking through a keyhole and seeing something that you didn't want to see. Her eyes were solemn, devoid of happiness—like she just didn't care.

That face—*my* face! I was stunned just looking at her. "I can't believe this. How is this possible?" I mouthed.

Habock said nothing. His eyes remained focused on her. He was staring at her neck.

We watched as the young woman picked up a rose-coloured book and placed it into a box filled with crimson tissue.

"Wait . . . that's my diary . . ."

He nodded.

The future me then closed the box and tied the ribbon tightly around it. She looked around the attic as if she were searching for an unexpected visitor. Perhaps she knew we were there watching her. She then placed the box on the floor and walked over to the window. There she stood, gazing up at the sky.

"I know what I have to do and I know that I need help to do it. Am I strong enough, though?" she said aloud.

I looked closely at her. The first thing I noticed when she entered the attic, was her clothes. She was dressed all in black. *Ick*, I thought.

This future vision of myself was depressing. Everything was black—*everything*. From her sweater to her shoes, all I saw was dark. Even the tight jewelled pieces around her neck were black, not a single ounce of colour surfaced from her.

Thinking about her outfit, I cringed. I would never wear something like that. For starters, my favourite colour was orange. No way would I ever be caught dead in such agonizing apparel. I felt sad just looking at her. This was definitely a darker version of myself. She reminded me of a black widow spider and so from that moment on, she became 'Black Scarlett'.

This couldn't possibly be me in the future. But then I had to remember that this wasn't me—not yet anyway. I wondered what could have possibly changed me so much in the past that I would want to look like this.

My attention was drawn to my right leg as I felt the onset of a major cramp. As I tried to reposition myself, my foot slipped away from my body and skidded along the floor.

Instantly, Black Scarlett looked over to where we were hiding. "Who's there?" she called out.

I could tell that Habock was not impressed with me divulging our presence. He shook his head at me and scolded me with his eyes.

"Sorry—I didn't mean to," I whispered.

It was too late for apologies. Black Scarlett was on her way over.

At that moment, something happened to me. I felt my chest tighten up as a fierce pain echoed through my heart. "Habock," I said, clenching my shirt.

The closer she got, the more it stung. "Ahh . . ."

"Who's there? Answer me!" she said, moving in.

With a single bound, Habock jumped out from behind the boxes. "Meow," he said.

I sat in place writhing in pain as he distracted her. *Get her away from me, Habock!*

"Whoa—nice kitty," she said, surprised. "What on Earth is a cat doing up in our attic?"

"Meow," he repeated a few times over.

"Aren't you pretty! You look like a Siamese. Now—be nice," I heard her say as I rocked back and forth with my arms wrapped around my body.

Their voices were moving away from the boxes. I could feel my chest starting to untwist as the pain slowly subsided. "Oh, thank God," I whispered to myself. That was scary. I had never had pains like that before. Right then and there, it got real for me—this was no dream. The moment Black Scarlett had moved towards me, my heart was under attack. Did Habock know that that would happen? He knew better than to mess with my heart. Maybe that's what he meant about us not seeing each other.

With deep breaths, I unlocked my limbs as I sat for a moment listening to the beats beneath my ribs. I could feel the normal drumming return. As I steadied myself, I peeked out to see where they were.

Like a trained dog, Black Scarlett followed Habock to the far side of the attic. The further away she moved, the better I felt.

"I don't know how you got up here, pretty girl . . . but you can't stay." She leaned over to pet him. Just as her fingers touched the edge of his furry coat, he spoke.

"Hello Scarlett," he said.

"WHOA WHOA WHOA!" she jumped back, screaming.

I couldn't help but roll my eyes behind the array of boxes. At least my reaction to the talking cat was a little more cool and collected. It seemed as though I had become more dramatic in the future. But then it occurred to me, why was she surprised? She knew all of this already. She knew Adonis was a talking cat and that his name was really Habock—this had already taken place in the past. What was going on here?

With my hand over my heart, I listened to their voices.

"Boy—you're kind of jumpy," Habock said, leaning his head to one side.

"What . . . . what are you?" Black Scarlett asked.

"I'm a cat of course. Oh, and by the way—I'm not a girl. So, if you don't mind, please don't call me 'pretty'. It's unflattering."

She just stared at him, mouth wide open.

"Apparently you haven't learned manners in the future either," he said with only a hint of arrogance. "My goodness, Scarlett, close your mouth—you're letting all the flies in. Okay, I'll start from the beginning. My name is Habock. I'm a talking cat and yes I'm in your attic . . . right now . . . in front of you."

"Habock? Your name is Habock?"

"Yes."

"Am I imagining this?" she said.

"No."

"You're in my attic . . . right now."

"Yes, Scarlett. I believe we've established that."

She looked down at him and scowled. "You're kind of pompous."

Habock seemed amused by the comment. His smile grew in merriment as he began to laugh aloud.

"Oh my God . . . you're laughing. There's a laughing cat in my attic right now. Can cats even laugh?"

"Why not—I like to laugh."

Looking out from behind the boxes, I could see that she was warming up to him. He had this undeniable charm that even the future me couldn't resist. Quietly, I sat and watched them.

"You've got to be kidding me," she said.

"Nope—no jokes."

Then her demeanour changed. Her shoulders lowered and she seemed to relax. With slow steps, she moved in to take a closer look at him.

"Wow, you're pretty cool. A talking cat—that's interesting. I've seen a lot of weird stuff these last few years but a talking cat—that's new."

Habock sat still like a temple statue. He observed her mannerisms with meticulous scrutiny.

"So, how do you know my name?" she asked.

"Well, actually Scarlett—I've known you for a long time now."

"Really? How long?"

"I'll tell you some other time. Are you feeling okay now? Do you believe what you see?" he said.

"I'm not sure. I think I do. You seem real." She reached out and touched his head as her fingers slid down along his silky back. Yep—you feel real."

He began to purr.

"You feel real, you sound real, you look real. I guess you're real."

"Good, I'm glad to hear it."

"Me too, I thought I was going crazy there for a minute."

"There's that word again—crazy. You keep using that word," Habock said, shaking his head.

"What do you mean? I just said that now. When did I use it before?"

"Um . . . nevermind. It's a thing of the past. But you could help me with something. You know what I'd really like right now?"

"No, what?"

"I'd like some food, I'm quite hungry. Do you have any tuna?"

"Yeah, I think so. We can go down to the kitchen and get you some," she said, turning towards the attic door.

"No, no. If you don't mind, I'd rather stay here. Could you bring it up to the attic?"

"Oh okay, Habock. Habock . . . that's a funny name. Don't go anywhere. I'll be right back, Habock—the talking cat," she smiled.

"Thank you, Scarlett."

With that, she left.

A moment later I popped my head out from behind the boxes. "Habock—what just happened?"

"You were almost discovered! That's what happened," he said in an angry tone. "You cannot let her find you—do you understand?"

"It wasn't intentional, you know. Besides, I'm the one who got hurt here," I said, patting my chest.

"Scarlett—this was not the plan." But when he saw the placing of my hand, he softened. "I'm sorry. It's just that I never told you about the consequences—they can be severe. Are you okay?"

"I am now but that was really scary. It was so strange. The closer she got to me, the more pain I felt. Look, I'm sorry that I made that noise but at least she didn't see me—she only saw you."

Habock frowned at me. "You must be careful from now on."

"I know, I know. I'm sorry. So what do we do now?"

"Well, we need to talk to her and find out more about the Mirrorwalkers."

"But I thought you already knew about them?"

"Yes, but we need to know how much *she* knows."

"Habock, I thought you just wanted to show me what I was like in the future. I've seen myself now—more than I wanted, actually. And if physical pain is one of the consequences, then I'd rather go home, thank you very much. Can't we just go back?" I said, hoping that this adventure would end here.

"It's not that easy, Scarlett. She knows about me now. I can't hide that. And if my instincts are right, then she won't be the only one to know. The knowledge of my presence in this time will soon spread. And then others will want to know why I have come. It won't be long before they find out."

"By 'others' do you mean the Mirrorwalkers?"

"Yes, and they will think that the future Scarlett is behind it."

"And then what? What will happen to her?"

Habock shook his head. "I don't know. We're going to have to find out." Then he paused.

"Habock—what is it?" I said.

"Hmm. I'm not sure. Something feels odd about all of this. It's just that you—the future you—seemed a little too accepting of my presence here. She was quite surprised when I first jumped out and spoke to her, yet she accepted me pretty quickly, don't you think?"

"Well, you were the one who said I had changed in the future," I offered. "And by the way—why doesn't she know about you? If we already met in the past and time continues on its merry way, then shouldn't she remember you?"

Habock didn't answer.

"*Well?*" I pried.

Habock wasn't listening to me. He was deep in thought. "Something feels a little off, I can't quite put my paw on it."

I laughed. "You know, you speak just like a person in a little cat body."

He looked up at me and smirked.

"Well, it's not an insult—I just think it's cute the way you talk."

Promptly, he jumped to another topic. "Now Scarlett, you must be gossamer-like. You don't exist here—you're not meant to. They will know about me, but you will be a mystery. Perhaps we will use that to our advantage."

"A mystery, eh? I can do that."

"Yes, like a puzzle. A ghostly puzzle. That's all you can be in this place—now that *I've* become a part of it."

I felt bad, knowing that the direction we were headed in was the direct result of my carelessness. "All this because my leg cramped up?"

"Yes, Scarlett. But fear not. We will fix this too." He peered up at me with a look of assurance and said, "All we need is some time."

FRIENDS OF NOW

ABOCK SAT ON his haunches as he finished off the last bit of tuna from the can. "Mmmm . . . there's nothing quite like tuna, except for Quarsfin that is."

Black Scarlett sat next to him on the floor, petting his silky coat. "Didn't they just discover that fish this year? You've tried it already?"

"Yes, it's a new find but when it comes to food—nothing stands in my way. I can get my paws on anything!"

"I see."

"Boy, that was good. Was that the last can?" he said, anxiously.

"Yes, Habock. That was the fifth and final can. Geez, my mom's gonna wonder where all the tuna went. What am I supposed to tell her?"

"Tell her you were feeding a stray in the backyard," he said, licking his lips. "Now where was I?"

"You were telling me about the future," she said, crossing her arms. "Not that it matters anyway. It is what it is. I don't know why you came here to tell me otherwise."

Behind the boxes I sat, trying not to fidget, as I listened to my future self. I only hoped that she would remain on the other side of the room. I was safest if she stayed there. Then I wondered—why didn't *she* show any signs of pain? I seemed to be the only Scarlett affected. That was a haunting thought.

Earlier, when Black Scarlett was downstairs retrieving Habock's tuna, I was upstairs, preparing for a more comfortable visit behind the cardboard jungle. I refused to let a leg cramp ruin my day and I didn't want to be the cause of any more problems. That, and I didn't want to be in anymore pain—I had learned *that* lesson the hard way.

I stretched my body out like a plank and propped my head up with my arms, as I prepared to tune into the conversation Habock was going to have with my future self. He said that he wanted me to focus on her movements, her voice and her change in expression. I guess he figured that I would know her better than anyone.

So there I sat in secret, hoping to learn more about myself.

"Scarlett, you look so lost," he said, his voice full of compassion. "Only you aren't."

His kindness hit a nerve.

Like a provoked pit viper, she struck back with fury. "How would you know? My sister hates me and my mom doesn't trust me anymore. My friends have abandoned me, what else is there? I'm trying to fight what has happened. But it's so hard when I'm all alone in a world that's dead set against me."

Habock shook his head. "Is that what you believe? Is that what *they* told you?"

"You mean my family? No, they didn't have to."

"That's not who I was referring to," he said.

In an instant, her manner changed. I watched as suspicion lifted her body off of the floor. Her head shifted to one side. I knew that look—she doubted his honesty. She seemed genuinely surprised to learn that Habock knew about her secret relationship with the Mirrorwalkers.

"How do you know about them?" she said, backing away.

"Scarlett—haven't you been listening to me? I'm from the future. I know what happens. I've seen more than you have, more than you'd want."

"What do you know of it!" she cried.

With vigilance, I examined her behaviour as she began to pace across the wooden floor. Her actions revealed a youthful desire, like a baby longing for its mother. I was no psychiatrist but I knew that feeling. It was confirmed when I saw the look in her eyes. And my gut was telling me that I was right. She craved love.

"Where were you then, when they first found me? Where were you when they turned my heart to stone? Where were you when my family cast me out as the bad child without a future?"

Habock didn't respond. He just let her weep.

"You have no idea what I've been through. My life is a constant battle. Not out there—but in here," she said, pointing to her heart. "So don't tell me that you've seen more than I have. I've seen more than my share and I can't look anymore." She turned and walked towards the window.

"Not even the moon will accept me anymore. I used to talk to her all the time. But now she has forsaken me."

"Avari sees everyone for who they really are, Scarlett. She knows what happened to you, she saw you in your darkest hours. Still, she believes in you."

Black Scarlett said nothing.

"And in your heart," he continued, "you've seen the side of hope. You are not alone in this fight, understand that."

Looking down with watery eyes, Black Scarlett shook her head. "How do you know all of this?"

"Because I know you—the *true* you. I know what happened the night of your sixteenth birthday party."

She turned her back to him and began sobbing. "I can't . . . please . . . no . . ."

All I heard were wet words. I wondered what they were talking about—what *wasn't* being said.

Habock quickly stepped in front of her. He was determined to reach her. "And I know you were manipulated because of the circumstances. The Mirrorwalkers turned you dark and you became one of them, until you escaped. But that's just not who you are anymore. Listen to your heart—what is it telling you?"

Her gaze fell to the floor. "It's telling me . . . that there is hope."

Habock captured her stare. "Then maybe you should trust it."

Black Scarlett nodded, silently.

"Deep inside, you know what to do. Be true to yourself, Scarlett. Do not renounce your inner being."

Finally, he broke through her guarded cover; a smile spread across her face. "You know, you speak just like a person in a little cat body."

Habock bobbed his head. "I know, I know, it's not an insult. It's just cute the way I talk, right?"

She wiped her eyes with the sleeve of her sweater. "Yeah—wait. How did you know I was going to say that?"

"It doesn't matter," he said.

"No—wait a minute. You said something earlier. You said that I used the word 'crazy' before, and now you knew what I was going to say before I even said it? How did you know that?"

Uh oh, I thought. *She's figuring it out.* I watched closely as Habock silently held his ground.

"You said that you knew about my future. But you knew I would come up here. And you know things about my past."

Habock, don't say it, I thought. Here I was trying to protect my future self from the past, when all I really wanted was to meet myself in the future. Still, I knew what Habock said was probably for the best. Letting my future self know too much would probably be a bad thing.

"You've been here before, haven't you?" she said.

Habock said nothing. He remained silent, unmoving.

I could see Black Scarlett, rationalizing, discovering and finally understanding the situation. "It's true, isn't it? You've been here before! That's how you knew I would come up here."

The cat was out of the bag—Black Scarlett was on to us. But then I had a mental pause. She didn't know about *me*. She had discovered Habock in the attic but she didn't know that *I* was here. Would she eventually find out?

Habock's silence was broken. "All you need to know is that I've travelled through time to help you. Right now, it doesn't matter where I've come from. What matters, is what we're going to do about the present."

She seemed surprised by his declaration. Like a mouse tossed between the paws of a playful cat, her mind appeared to be toying with this new information.

When I looked back at Habock, he was staring at Black Scarlett's neck. I wondered what it was that he found so enthralling. Then, out of nowhere came a question that I hadn't expected.

"Scarlett—there's something you need to tell me. Where did you get that necklace?" His tone was earnest.

In a protective manner, she lifted her hand to cover the band of triangular stones. "My necklace? That's an odd question to ask."

Habock was hell-bent on retrieving an answer. "I need to know—who gave it to you?"

"Okay, okay. Gwen did. Mom and Dad gave her the stones a few years ago and she made a necklace for me. She gave it to me a couple of days before we turned sixteen—as an early birthday present. She was upset that one of the jewels was broken but I didn't care."

Habock's response was pensive. "I see."

"Why are you asking me this? Are you going to tell me that my parents robbed a jewellery store or something?"

It was weird watching my reaction. I still couldn't believe that this was really me. A good chunk of me still doubted what was happening. How could I possibly be there and here at the same time? I waited for the inevitable pinch to waken me from this bizarre dream. Instead, the pinch came verbally as Habock redirected the conversation.

"Scarlett, there's someone that we need to see."

With sceptic eyes, she glared at him.

"You know who I mean; we need to talk to her."

Her? I thought. Who's 'her'? Who are they talking about?

Black Scarlett shook her head in disagreement.

"I'm not taking 'no' for an answer. We need to go now. We'll talk on the way there."

I was hoping that I'd heard him wrong. Did he just say that he was leaving? I didn't like the sound of that at all.

"I can't," she said.

Habock leapt onto the windowsill. "Yes, yes you can. Come on—we're going for a little walk."

"I don't think that that's a good idea, Habock. Besides, what would I say?"

"Say what's in your heart."

"You expect me to just drop everything and go right now? That's crazy!"

"No, what's crazy is that you're fighting me on this. You're being too hard on yourself, Scarlett. It's time that you let go of your inner demons."

She paused for a moment. "You really want me to do this?"

"Yes, I do," he said. "Now, get ready, we're going to see a friend."

GOING SOMEWHERE

ABOCK AND BLACK Scarlett were preparing to leave. Where they were headed—I had no idea.

Anxiously, I gazed out from behind the cardboard, trying to catch Habock's eye. I didn't want to be left alone in this time—I didn't belong here.

Habock sat perched on the windowsill, waiting for my future self to join him as they prepared to depart.

"What about my diary?" she said.

"Leave it—there's no use in hiding the box. I'm sure the Mirrorwalkers will soon find out about my arrival. And when they do, they'll find the diary no matter where you've hidden it. Your knowledge will soon be their knowledge," he said, gazing down at the yard.

Looking back, he hurried her. "Come on, Scarlett, we haven't got all day. We must get to Blue Beacon."

"I don't think she wants to see me, Habock."

"Come now, you must stop this. What happened in the past—must stay there. You've got to move on. It's time for you to confront the present. Let's go," he said, without pause. Habock wasn't giving her an inch. Damn, he was determined.

"Avari is noble and knowledgeable. She will have the answers. Trust me, she hasn't given up on you."

Black Scarlett sighed. "Okay, I'll go. But there is one problem."

"Which is?" he asked.

It sounded to me like she was stalling.

"If we leave, we can't go downstairs, Gwen will see us. She's the Gestapo around here and right now I'm on house arrest—I've been grounded."

"Then we'll have to climb out the window and down the side of the house. We'll use the trellis."

She gave an awkward laugh. "You're kidding right? Do you know how high up we are? What if I fall? I'm not climbing out that window. Plus, it's December—it's freezing outside and my jacket is downstairs."

Now, she really was stalling and I'm sure that Habock sensed it too. But the more I listened to him, the more I realized how good he was at encouraging others.

"*You*, Scarlett—afraid of falling? That's funny. Who's the one who crawls through the bedroom window almost every night? I've seen you climb. You're quite the cat yourself. Besides, you know very well that it's mild out. Now—stop dawdling."

She stood there for a moment. "But what if I fall?"

With those words, I finally understood what was wrong with my future self—her confidence had been stripped away. Her beliefs and her hope had been taken. And fear was what replaced it.

"I won't let you fall, you can trust me. I need you to do this. Please—we have to go," he said, tapping the glass. "Open the window."

His pleading worked.

"Oh God, I can't believe that I'm doing this. Okay, wait just a minute. If I'm going out there, then I at least need a jacket or something."

I quivered for a moment when I heard the wood creaking in my direction. *Oh no.* I held my body tight as I braced for another onset of heart pains. For here I was, this strange twin in time, hiding like a mouse behind the household memories.

The footsteps stopped as Habock called out to her. "Scarlett—no! Check this box here, there might be something in it."

The sound of her shoes gliding over the wood, headed in the other direction.

Thank you, Habock. I poked my head up to see what she was doing.

Black Scarlett opened the top of a large box and breezed through a pile of old clothing. I recognized it at once—it was one of Uncle Frankie's boxes.

"It's a little big but it'll do," she said, throwing a coat over her shoulders. She walked over to the window and unlatched the two brass locks at the top. Slowly, her arms pushed the glass upward as the cool air quickly filled the room. "Here goes nothing."

I watched as her legs passed through the window. Her body then disappeared outside.

Habock observed as she descended down the wooden trellis. He then looked back at me. "Scarlett—I need you to remain here until I get back."

"Where are you going? You can't leave me here alone—what am I supposed to do?"

"I have to take the future you to Blue Beacon to see Avari. It's important that I do this."

My thoughts were silenced as I played his words over and over again in my mind. *Avari . . .*

Avari. Then it clicked. "The *moon*? You're going to see the *moon*?"

"Yes."

"Seriously? I can't believe this!"

"I won't be gone long, I promise. Now—remember what I said about being here? You now know how important that is. The only thing I want you to do is read the diary—but stay hidden. Wait for me here."

I stared at him with panic in my eyes but said nothing.

"You'll be fine," he said, sensing the fear in my expression.

Then the words came back to me. "But what if . . ."

"No if's—you'll be fine. But whatever you do, do not leave this room!"

"Okay, I got it! Please hurry. Don't leave me here forever."

With that, he quickly moved through the window. The last thing I saw was his skinny black tail. Then he was gone.

Slowly I stood, stretching my body in all directions. I had remained this entire time concealed behind the fortress of boxes trying not to expose myself. It felt great to finally move. I tiptoed across the floor toward the window and looked down at the backyard. I searched the grass for Odin but he wasn't outside. Habock must have known that.

I watched as my intrepid little feline jumped from the trellis to the ground. Then together, he and Black Scarlett headed for the road.

Turning back, I saw the box with red ribbon sitting on the floor. I still couldn't believe that my diary was inside of it.

"Great—now I'm alone in the future. This'll be boring."

As I sat down and opened the box, I realized that I couldn't have been more wrong.

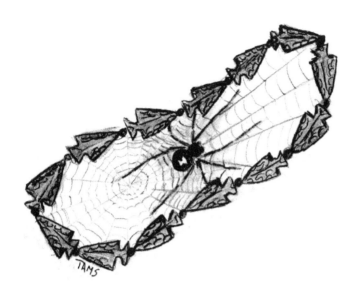

MORE TO LEARN

HAT PLAYED OUT before me was unbelievable. I was reading the entries in the diary, but the words were being read aloud like a book on tape. It was a talking diary, where all the pages came to life as you turned them. It was amazing.

Each entry was spoken by the person who wrote it, Black Scarlett in most cases. There were a few places however, where a young man's voice was audible.

I came across some of my old entries from two-and-a-half years ago which reassured me that this was indeed my diary—in case I had any lingering doubts. Hearing my voice come alive from back then seemed somewhat surreal, especially since I was sitting here in the future listening to it.

I was now concentrating on a conversation that took place on August 15, 2011 between Black Scarlett and a young man named Sparks. Carefully, I listened as the words played out—like little verbal theatrical scenes.

"Tell me everything you know about the Mirrorwalkers," Sparks said.

"Okay, here's what I know," Black Scarlett answered. "They're immortal night crawlers. They belong to the band of 'The Gypsy Sands'—relentless hunters in search of time. They surface at night and rise only during a

waxing moon—on the days nearest to the full one. They need the ligh
of the moon to move above ground. The remainder of their time is spen
below ground in a cave somewhere inside Finlake Forest."

"Is that everything?"

"No, not even close," she said. "They're searching for three powerfu
mirrors, and time is precious to them, which is why they must act quickly
during their leader's rise."

"When is that?"

"December 19th, 2012—under the first light of the Spider Moon," she
answered. "It's a lunar event that occurs only once every seven hundred
years."

"A Spider Moon?" Sparks asked.

"Yeah, it's based on mythology. Greco-Roman mythology states that
the mortal, Arachne, was turned into a spider. She had boasted that her
weaving skills were better than the Goddess Athena's. They had a weave-off
to compare their talents. Athena then destroyed Arachne's tapestry and
loom out of envy and slashed her face. Arachne then hung herself with a
rope. Athena turned Arachne into a spider and the noose into a web where
she could spin forever."

"Interesting . . ."

"The Mirrorwalkers believed that Arachne's power as a constellation
could be harnessed during that full moon. So they made a pact with
Arachne: if she helped them, then Venus or Aphrodite—the Goddess of
beauty—would help restore Arachne to the woman she once was. Aphrodite
took pity on Arachne and joined in the union."

"What about Athena?" he asked.

"Arachne, no doubt, will want revenge on Athena."

"That's crazy!"

"I know," Black Scarlett said.

"Okay, so what do they plan on doing?"

"During the three phases of the full moon, the moon, Earth and Venus
will all be in direct line of sight with Arachne's constellation. The sun's
light will cast a shadow off of Venus and Earth, placing a shape onto the
moon—a spider. The stars from Arachne's constellation will light the path
as the animal crawls across the moon's surface. From Earth, it'll look like a
spider crossing the moon."

Sparks was silent.

"So, let's go back to the Leader. He will rise on the 19th and then send
his minions in to occupy the triangle of forests: Blazenridge, Finlake Fir and

Grinstone Gail. Now, unless he has all three mirrors, he will not control the forests."

I couldn't believe what I was hearing. Although I was sitting comfortably on the attic floor, part of me felt as though I was inside a classroom. What impressed me the most however, was my future knowledge of the subject matter. *How did I know all this stuff?*

Nose to the book, I listened.

"If they find all three mirrors, then the Leader will have control over the forests as he will be able to harness their elements. Once Blazenridge is set afire, he will march to Velvet Elm. If he succeeds in getting there, then his power over the Elms will be the end of the fight. Velvet Elm is the hub of goodness. It sits in the heart of the triangle of forests. It's the last remaining place of hope. He will tap into the Elms' power which will allow Arachne to weave her web around Avari," Black Scarlett said.

"Why Velvet Elm, though? What's he after?" Sparks said.

"At the centre of the forest stands the Tree of Life. It's the oldest tree in the woods, roughly seven hundred years old. At the top of the tree lies a golden web. Arachne, in the form of a spider, will use the power of the web to weave one last tapestry."

"Oh no . . . they're going to use the web against Avari?"

"Yes."

"But what do they want with her?"

"Ultimately, they want to capture her light so they can surface at any time during the lunar cycle. That means they'll have more time above ground to forge their power and change the world. If Arachne paralyzes Avari, then capturing her light will be easy. Avari will eventually be destroyed and the Earth will no longer have a moon. The Mirrorwalkers will control the night, and with all three mirrors they will eventually control time."

"We can't let that happen, Scar!"

"Trust me, I know."

"Okay—tell me more about the Leader."

"Well, his grave lies inside Finlake Forest—where you found me—beneath the Silver Flint. It's in the cave where the Mirrorwalkers are. They're awaiting his release from the Forest Creeper—a tree inside the cave, with roots that move. It's really eerie. Each root of the tree operates individually and believe me when I tell you, it's incredibly smart. The Leader's grave is wrapped inside the Creeper's roots."

"Did you see his grave?"

"No, they wouldn't let me see it," Black Scarlett said. "Oh, and one more thing—everything is under sand."

"*Sand*—in the forest?"

"Gypsy sands, actually. They call it 'Gypsy' because the sand moves mysteriously around the forest, which means that the cave moves as well. The Mirrorwalkers are all part of the Gypsy Sands. Everything they do is secretive, completely hidden so that no one will find them."

"Is that everything you learned while you were there?" Sparks asked.

"I think so, but there are certain things that I can't remember. Like, how to get back there, and what the cave looks like. Part of my memory is missing—I don't know what they did to my head. I do know that once the Leader rises, his first order of business will be to take the forests. So, if we can get there before that happens then we might stand a chance . . ." she trailed off.

"Scar—what is it?"

"I don't know. I have this feeling . . . that we're being watched. I'm sorry Sparks but I have to go."

"Wait—Scar," he said.

That's where the conversation ended. I waited a moment, so to break myself away from their multi-layered tale of written events. The diary was fascinating but so much information was being thrown around. My head was starting to hurt. I wondered why Habock had wanted me to read this.

The line between fiction and non-fiction was starting to disappear as tales of truth and legends of fables began to coalesce. Instead of categorizing them as blocks or pieces of information, I decided to focus solely on the storyline—no matter how bizarre it seemed.

As I turned the page, both voices started up again under a new date—September 1, 2012.

"You know, Scar, I've been thinking. There's a possibility that the Leader *is* already here. I mean . . . what if he never was at rest? What if he's been here the whole time?"

"Why would you say that? I don't believe that!" she said, her voice obstinate.

"Come on . . . we have to at least consider the possibility. You never saw his grave while you were underground and there are some things that just don't make any sense."

"I know, but still I don't want to think that. Look, we need to focus on the mirrors. The Mirrorwalkers have found two of them and now they're looking for the third, the one that belongs to the remaining Kingdom of the Cats.

I closed the book for a moment to mentally soak in all the information that was just read to me. Most of the puzzle pieces were still scattered in my mind but a couple of them were starting to fit together. I looked back at the velvet-covered frame and thought, *Is this the mirror they're talking about? Habock's mirror?*

Just then, I heard a noise from across the room. To me it sounded like the hissing of a cat. It was very subtle though, hardly noticeable. Had the room not been quiet, I might not have heard it. My eyes searched for movement of any kind but there wasn't any.

I was then distracted by the light beaming through the window. It suddenly occurred to me that it was getting late in the day. A rosy hue entered the glass as the sun lowered itself from the sky.

It felt like I had been in the attic for days. I was alone with my thoughts, the same way I had started the day. It seemed somewhat strange to be here by myself and yet it was still my attic, so I wasn't too uncomfortable.

My mind was ready to move ahead. As I opened the book, the voices began to speak.

"All they need is that third mirror, then they'll have control of the forests," Black Scarlett said.

"We can't let them find that third mirror, Scar."

"I know, I know. But there's only two of us. We can't stop them until we have a third—a reflection of me. 'One of strength to bind; two identical of power'—that's what the prophecy says. We need a third to form the Triangle of Might. It's supposed to be Gwen but I can't ask her—I just can't. I don't ever want her to know about this."

"We'll figure it out, Scar. Maybe there's another way," Sparks said, calmly.

Just as the sentence ended, the pages began to flip forward on their own, as if an imaginary breeze was blowing them. "What the . . ."

I stuck my hand inside the book to stop the pages from moving. I found the entry I had just listened to and started skimming the words. Just as the voices started up, the pages began to flip again, this time stopping on a blank sheet. My eyes grew wide as letter by letter, words began to appear on the page. One by one, the words turned into sentences as a new voice appeared in the book. And I knew at once whose voice it was—Habock's.

The date 'December 19th, 2012' suddenly popped up in the top right corner. It was today's date. I realized that not only was this a talking diary—it was a self-writing one too. This book was incredible.

Right now, a new conversation was formulating onto the page. I could hear the dialogue between Habock and Black Scarlett as they headed for Blue Beacon. I, of course, was familiar with this park as I had been there many times in the past. This was neat though—it was as if I was right there beside them, invisibly listening to their words as each syllable poured out of their mouths. And into my ears, their conversation sank.

"I told you, it doesn't matter anymore. We tried everything," Black Scarlett said.

"It *does* matter, Scarlett, and you know it. Help will come. You've pleaded for it and now it's here."

"Wait . . . you read my diary? No one was supposed to find that. It was meant for . . ."

"I know who it was meant for. And believe me, she found it," Habock said.

Oh wow, they were talking about me. No way was I going to miss this. I was a high school student; eavesdropping on conversations was normal—heck, it was expected. Okay, so maybe this wasn't the typical 'what on Earth is she wearing, he's so cute, let's cut class' teenage rant, but it didn't matter. They were talking about me. My mind was alert.

"I don't believe it!" Black Scarlett said with surprise. "It worked? That was my last shot at changing all of this. I didn't know where else to turn."

"But you knew that that would happen. You must have known that I was going to the past. How else would your diary have made it there?" Habock paused. "You knew I would bring it to her."

Black Scarlett admitted her secret. "Yes, I knew. But wait a minute—how is that possible? I just packaged it up when you arrived. It's still in the attic."

"Well, you see," Habock explained, "this event has already taken place. The mirror allowed me to move through time at my own speed. I simply left my time, stopped here along the way and brought your diary with me to the past. This happened fifteen years ago."

Black Scarlett had this confounded quietness about her. I didn't have to be there to see it—I could just tell. Perhaps she was baffled. I know I was. This mess of tangled time was starting to give me a headache.

Habock continued. "For my visit today, I came from the past to *your* present in the hopes of saving everyone's future. You'll understand one day."

"Okay," she said. "I don't know if I grasped all of that, but regardless, I knew you would come. When the Mirrorwalkers took me, I overheard them talking about your arrival—a cat traveling through time. I just didn't know when that would be. Then Sparks saved me from them and brought me home. I thought maybe a time traveling cat could help me," she said.

"How did Sparks find you?"

"I had just escaped the cave when everything disappeared behind me. Sparks said that he found me wandering around Finlake Forest. He said that when he first saw me, I was really out of it. He saw nothing else."

Habock was quiet.

"So, I take it you've met the Mirrorwalkers before."

"You could say that." Habock's tone was condescending and bitter. "They are the rulers, the dictators of the future. They call themselves Kings, but deserve neither the honour nor the designation. And you Scarlett—are their pawn."

"There's nothing more I can do. The diary was my last shot. I mean, Sparks helped me out a lot but now we're both stuck and tonight's the night."

"Hmm . . . you said that you didn't know when I would arrive?"

"That's right," she answered.

"Then something's wrong—I can feel it. Tell me about the three forests—Finlake Fir, Grinstone Gail and Blazenridge."

"All three are now occupied by the Mirrorwalkers," she said.

"Are you sure?" he stressed.

"Yes."

"Then the Leader has risen, and time should now be our main focus. But something tells me that he was already here."

"No—that can't be! I didn't think that was possible!"

I could tell by the tone of Black Scarlett's voice that she was incredibly upset by this news, as if someone had pulled the proverbial rug out from beneath her. Her foundation was shaken.

"It's the only way I see it," Habock said. "But we haven't lost the battle yet. The Mirrorwalkers may have taken the forests, but none are yet in their hands. Blazenridge is not lit—I would know if it was."

There was a break in the conversation, it seemed as though their words had come upon a roadblock. *What were they doing?* I wondered. Then my ears stirred at the sound of my sister's name.

"Scarlett, have you talked to Gwen about any of this?"

"No. She'd just try to think of more ways to save me. You know, Habock I'm not the only one who's changed around here. She's turned into Miss Goody Two-Shoes. She only makes me feel worse when I'm around her. I don't want her to know about any of this."

I listened for Habock's response but to my surprise, he didn't have one. Instead, he rephrased the question.

"Are you *sure* Gwen doesn't know what's going on?"

"I'm sure—she knows nothing. She still thinks that Sparks is a bad guy. But he's one of us, he's on our side."

"I know," he said. "Well, Scarlett, this is your lucky day because *I* am going to help you. And it seems that I've arrived just in time."

"*You're* gonna help me? No offense but you're very little . . . and . . . a cat . . . and well . . ."

"Now, now—that's not the attitude. I'll have you know that I have more tricks up my sleeve than you can shake a stick at."

I laughed at his response from inside the attic. That was something my father would have said. But his phrasing was the key—it was working away at Black Scarlett's downtrodden spirit. He was that glimmer of hope that she desperately sought.

"You're really gonna help me?"

"Oh—I'll do more than that. Together, you and I are going to save the future." I could hear the strength in his voice. He sounded like Superman.

"You must have a lot of faith in me, Habock."

"Scarlett, my dear—you have no idea!"

OBJECT OF DESIRE

HE PREVIOUS CONVERSATION between Habock and Black Scarlett seemed to end on a high note. The last few minutes however were quiet, no words were written. Both of them had remained silent during the last stretch of their walk.

My attention was again drawn to the window as I watched the vast array of colours dance in the sky. I felt like they were putting on a show for me. This playful performance of Nature seemed tactile—as if I could reach out and touch it. With each beat of my heart, I could see the sky moving closer. The rainbow of air was infiltrating my skin as my mother's face came in and out of view. She was mouthing something to me but her words were stifled by silence.

Suddenly, I was plucked out of my trance as words began to reappear on the page.

"I brought the mirror with me to the past, Scarlett, so I could protect it," Habock said.

"Then why haven't I seen it? And why haven't we met before today?" Black Scarlett said.

I could tell by her breathing that they were still walking.

Habock's answer was quick. "You *have* seen it, Scarlett. We *have* me before. You don't remember me because part of your memory was erased by the Mirrorwalkers."

"It's because of what happened the night of my party, isn't it?"

"It's not just that. The Mirrorwalkers have been strategically timing themselves in preparation for their rise to power. All they need is that third mirror. Then they can move through time and space and change anything they want—past, present and future. You know this already. Think of it: what if Napoleon hadn't been defeated at Waterloo? What if the Bubonic Plague had reached the shores of North America? What if Christopher Columbus had never crossed the Atlantic? These immortal creatures will play with the fabric of time to achieve their goals."

"They can't do that!" I said aloud, from my seat in the attic. I was in total disbelief. "That's impossible—no one has the power to go back in time and change events like that! Habock, you're crazy!" I felt like a cuckoo yelling at the book, especially since I was the only one in the room. Had I been standing alongside Habock and Black Scarlett, then I would have had an audience. I refused to adhere to such ridiculous statements. But regardless of the story, I continued to listen.

Habock forged ahead. "Tell me something, what if penicillin hadn't been discovered? What if the Berlin Wall had never come down? What if the United Nations was never founded? What if the Cuban Missile Crisis hadn't been resolved? This is what they want those mirrors for. They want to rule their own world."

Black Scarlett didn't say anything. I was the one doing all the talking. "Okay, now I've heard it all." And then I thought of something—if Black Scarlett knew this, then why was Habock describing it to her? Is this why he wanted me to read the diary—so that *I* could learn something from it? Was he saying this for me?

"Now, let's try a more personal approach." He paused for a moment. "How would you feel if something bad happened to someone else in your family? And what if you couldn't prevent that event because you weren't there to stop it?"

I was blindsided by his words. *Someone else? What was that supposed to mean?* My thoughts were thrown across the attic as I scrambled to collect them.

Again, Black Scarlett said nothing.

"Do you see my point now? These are things they will do if they find that third mirror. They needed you to tell them where it was. The rest, they removed from your mind. Scarlett—they washed away your memories of hope. That's why you don't remember me. To you—I was just some stray cat who showed up in your house one day."

"You were a pet, that's what they told me."

"I figured as much. They knew better of course, and probably assumed that one day I would lead them to the mirror. But that never happened and you never told them about it either," Habock said.

"How do you know that?"

"Because the mirror was cloaked, hidden from view. Only you and I could see it. I put a spell on you so you wouldn't reveal its location."

"Then why did you cover it?" she asked.

"I needed to hide it from you, until you were ready to know the truth. The Mirrorwalkers are obviously still looking for it. And you know as well as I do, how much they need it, especially on this night. They've caused a lot of pain in your past, Scarlett—more than you know. And for two reasons—they wanted you and that mirror."

"What are you saying, Habock? That *they* caused the accident?"

I shook my head as I tried to understand what they were talking about. *What accident? Whose accident?*

"Are you saying it wasn't me? That *they* were the ones who . . ." Black Scarlett trailed off. "No . . ."

Habock tried to console her. "Come back to me, Scarlett. Remember, if we succeed in all of this, then *that* future won't exist anymore. I promise—we're going to change all of this."

I could hear Black Scarlett whimpering, but by Habock's response I could tell that she was in accordance with him.

"That's good, I'm glad you believe me," he said. "You know that the other two mirrors have been found, so we must do everything we can to protect this one—they mustn't find it."

I sat still as a board in the attic, listening to his voice. I now knew exactly what they were talking about. The large oval frame behind me wasn't holding just any mirror—it was holding *the* mirror.

"Let me tell you what really happened," Habock said. "In the beginning, the mirrors belonged to three Kingdoms: the mighty Batfish who protected the seas, the giant Sparrowhawks who protected the skies and the noble Cats who protected the land."

"And you were one of them," Black Scarlett guessed.

"Yes. My family of Siamese lived among them. My father rescued the baby belonging to the Queen Lynx Armandia. He almost drowned in a river but my father saved him from his death. The mirror was given to my father as the highest honour from the Queen. And there he vowed to protect it. And for many years, he did.

"We learned that the mirror was highly desired by the Mirrorwalkers—they came quite close to finding it. They sought to use it for their own domination. After the Kingdom's walls had been breached, I was secretly sent to the past to keep it safe. The decision was made that I would watch over you *and* the mirror until the time came for us to help each other."

"How did you know that I was involved with them? Why did I need to be watched over?" Black Scarlett's voice sounded genuinely innocent.

"You, Scarlett, were the one standing next to the Mirrorwalkers when our Kingdom was overthrown. *You* were the one who was sent in to look for the mirror."

"Me?"

"Yes. It was December 19th, 2012, the day that the Leader rose from his grave. He summoned you from your home and you went willingly."

Her tone was bleak. "I did that?"

"Think back," Habock said. "Did you ever wonder about *how* you escaped from the Mirrorwalkers cave? And how easy it was for Sparks to find you? It was all part of their master plan. They *let* you escape—they released you."

"No—" she said.

"Yes, Scarlett, it's true. When this happened before, Sparks wasn't there to find you. You found your own way back. You were programmed to return to the Mirrorwalkers on the day that the Leader rose. That's when they turned you against everything good. They preyed on the weakness in your heart, and you returned to join them."

Oh no! I thought. It was more than what Habock had told me. I felt like I was being verbally pummelled from all sides of the room. Somehow, I had become this tragic monster in the future; one that was aligned with harmful beings. *I* was the thing that Habock was trying to stop.

Every inch of my body shivered in denial as I tried frantically to rid my mind of evil thoughts. "You're not evil, you're not evil—it's just a story . . ." I told myself, over and over again. But how much more of this fantasy was I supposed to take before I succumbed to its validity?

As much as I tried to convince myself that Habock's words were simply illusion, the story was becoming more concrete with each breath I took. And that's what scared me the most.

"What you don't know, Scarlett, is that when I was sent to the past, I knew some things had to change. You needed help—another person that you could talk to. For that, I recruited Sparks. You and he were a lot alike—I knew you'd be good for one another. I only hoped that he'd be there for you in your time of need. And it seems as though my plan has worked."

"But what about tonight—I'm supposed to go back tonight!" she said.

"Well, that's why I came—to make sure that you didn't go back to the Mirrorwalkers. Now Sparks and I are both here to stop that from happening," he finished.

Why that sneaky little cat, I thought. He told me that he hadn't expected to get caught by Black Scarlett. Boy was he a good actor. Now I knew why he came on this day. It made me think about what other surprises he had in store for me.

"But Habock—what about spies?" Black Scarlett continued. "They must have spies looking for that mirror."

"Yes . . . many, actually—all creatures of the natural world. They were sent to all areas of the Earth: deserts, plains, seas, oceans and skies. Robberflies and Gobblinsharks were sent to the skies and seas, respectively. And for my mirror they sent in their most powerful weapon—the Scarlett King Cobra. And it's still looking for the mirror."

"Wait a minute . . . are you telling me that there's a snake out there with my name looking for the mirror—the one that's sitting in the attic?"

"Yes, but remember the mirror is cloaked. Only you and I can see it," he said.

"But what about right now? We're talking about it right now."

"Yes, but look where you are, Scarlett."

I assumed that she became aware of her surroundings by the silent pause in their conversation.

"It's Blue Beacon—we're here!" she said.

"This forest is protected by Avari's light and so is the land surrounding it. No one can hear us."

Oh wow, I thought. *They went to talk to the moon, Habock wasn't kidding.* I couldn't believe that the moon was really alive. It would have been interesting to see that.

"What about the Leader?" Black Scarlett asked. "Can he hear us?"

"No, not even he can," Habock answered, "even if he *has* been here all along."

Black Scarlett was quiet. Her voice returned a moment later, shaken. " still don't understand how that's possible."

"There's only one explanation I can think of and it hurts me to say it."

She must have understood the graveness in his tone. "Then you should take the mirror back with you, get it away from here. You're not safe around me, Habock. Oh God—what about the cobra?"

I gasped. It finally hit me. The hissing noise I heard earlier—it wasn't just my imagination. At that moment the first wave of fear hit my body. Here I was in another time, in the attic all alone. And somewhere out there was a poisonous snake looking for this mirror. And I had a sickening feeling that he was closer than I thought. Now I knew who the hiss belonged to.

Slowly, I looked behind me at the fabric covering the frame. "Oh no!" I now felt completely unsafe sitting there, and I was pretty sure that my mother's knitting needles weren't going to protect me this time. My prayers were simple: Please don't let that reptile show up while I'm here alone!

I soon realized however, that a mirror-seeking snake would be the least of my worries. I was about to be discovered by something else.

LOST AND FOUND

CLOSED THE diary and slid it across the floor. It landed behind some old household items where I hoped no one would find it.

Someone was climbing the ladder, heading for the attic. I searched for the closest place to hide, but it was too late. I made it as far as the open clothing box in the corner when I saw Gwen's head appear in the room. I froze, thinking that my stillness might hide me.

"Scarlett—what are you doing up here?" she glared at me.

I didn't know what to say. I was speechless. I was just as surprised as she was, really. For here she was two-and-a-half years older, and me from two-and-a-half-years in the past. She would know that this wasn't the right Scarlett. Mind you, she looked pretty much the same. She wasn't smiling though and that was noticeably different. But the more I thought about it, the more I realized—*I* didn't look that much different in the future either. Maybe this *would* work.

The words dangled on my tongue. "I . . . um . . . well . . . you caught me."

"Caught you? Doing what, exactly?" she said.

"Well, since I *am* grounded . . . I thought I would come up to the attic and clean. Yep, that's what I was doing." I had no idea if she was going to buy any of this but since I had already been found, I figured I could do a little acting.

"What are you wearing?"

Oh no, my clothes. I forgot about my clothes.

"I thought you only wore black now, Miss Princess of Darkness. You look good with some colour. It's nice to see you like this."

I looked down at my green-striped shirt, blue jeans and orange Converse sneakers. "Oh . . . right," I said, my words stunted. "I was . . . just trying on some things from this box here." I pointed to the stack of clothing beside me. "There's some really neat stuff in here . . . like this jacket," I said, grabbing the nearest item on top. Playfully, I threw it over my shoulders. It was quite large; I felt like I was swimming in it.

Gwen smiled at me. "I didn't realize that you enjoyed wearing Uncle Frankie's clothes. He's only a hundred pounds heavier than you but hey . . . to each his own."

My true colours were showing and that was the problem. My future self had no colour. I had to fix this, so I tried to divert Gwen's attention away from my wardrobe. "Do you . . . need me for something?"

"Yeah, Scar. Mom wants to talk to you. It's probably about Sparks. Be in the kitchen in five."

Okay, now it was time to panic. Habock specifically told me not to leave this room. I could feel my heartbeat quickening. Why oh why did I have to get up and walk around? Why couldn't I have just read the diary behind the boxes? Habock was going to kill me when he came back.

"Scar—are you listening to me?"

"Um . . . yes. I mean, yeah—I heard you the first time. I'm not deaf you know!" I said jumping into my future attitude. I had to be careful, I couldn't be too nice.

"In five," Gwen said, stepping down the ladder, her face disappearing.

Good grief, what have I done? As I rationalized the last few minutes in my head, I began to pace across the floor. I dropped my hands into the pockets of the jacket and winced in pain as my right index finger touched something sharp. "Ouch," I said, pulling it out. A small trickle of blood appeared on the tip of my finger. I looked at the cut and then wiped the blood on my jeans. It took less than a minute for the wound to heal, which was a good thing since I couldn't stand the sight of blood. Not even my own.

Looking down, I noticed something glassy at the bottom of the pocket. I took off the jacket, placed it on the floor and turned the pocket inside out. Onto the floor fell a jagged piece of dark glass. It was small, roughly two inches long.

Gently, I picked it up. Although it was light in my hand, I felt a strong force emanating from it. Bathed in a stream of ebony, I couldn't help but be drawn to it. It reminded me of something I had seen before.

I was so mesmerized by the tiny object, that I hadn't noticed the envelope that fell out after it. A moment later I saw it. *What's this?* I wondered. Unsealed, I opened it. There, in my Uncle Frankie's hand writing was a letter addressed to me; it was dated July 7th 2008. I had never received this letter. This was the first time I'd laid eyes on it.

Thinking back, I remembered. That was the day my uncle was taken to the nursing home. How could I forget—it was such a depressing day. Mom, Dad and Gwen took him there that afternoon, while I stayed at home. I couldn't bear the thought of my favourite uncle being stuck in a place like that—he was only forty-three years old for Pete's sake. My heart wouldn't let me be part of the welcoming committee.

I remembered how we took most of the things from his apartment and put them up in the attic. It was a damn sad day.

Gazing down at the letter in my hand, I sighed. I didn't want to read it but when I saw the words, *Siamese cat,* I knew right there what I had to do. But as I started to read, I heard my mother call for me.

Immediately, I slipped the jewel into the envelope and stuffed the package inside my pants pocket. I threw the jacket aside.

I forgot that my mother wanted to see me. Great, now I had to come up with a plan and a good one at that. Playing me was the easy part. Pretending to be someone I wasn't, was difficult. There was no way out of this and my time was up.

"Pick one Scarlett," I told myself, "and run with it!"

OLD AND NEW

"SO, YOU'RE TELLING me that you just decided to go up to the attic and start cleaning? Really, Scarlett—is that the best you can do?" My future mother said, staring at me from across the kitchen.

Her cross-examination of me had become increasingly disturbing in the future. She was reluctant to give me any benefit of the doubt and in the first five minutes of our conversation I understood the severity of her stare. There was no trust in me—the *future* me that is. I guess I had blown that mutual respect thing we had going.

My thoughts were dispersed throughout my head; I was busy trying to figure out what sort of monster I had become, while trying to stay calm as I answered her questions. I didn't belong here, but because I had been discovered in the attic I had to deal with this. Once again, I was required to fix a problem that I had created, single-handedly. Man, Habock was going to blow a fuse.

And so here I was, sitting in the kitchen, two-and-a-half years down the road with my mother—the bloodhound—on my trail. She was a smart lady and would soon sniff me out. I had to be extremely careful about what I said.

"Yes, I was. It was messy . . . . and needed to be cleaned. What's the problem?" I said, nonchalantly.

"The problem is Sparks. I told you, Scarlett, that I don't want you talking to that boy—he's bad news. If I'd known it was him on the phone—I would have hung up."

"Why? What did he do that was so bad?" My look of surprise was genuine. I honestly didn't know what she was talking about.

"We've had this discussion before. I want you to stay away from him."

"But Mom, why don't you like him?" Now I was fishing for information. Was he part of the Mirrorwalkers band? Habock and my future self didn't seem to think so but perhaps they had been misled.

"You know, Scarlett, I can't quite put my finger on it but something's different about you."

My lips froze and my tongue was at a standstill. I had no answer for this question and no clever retort to help me escape it.

"Your clothes are different but that's not it." Slowly, she approached me. "There's something about your face . . . you look different somehow."

Uh oh, I thought. *Is she on to me? How could she possibly know?*

My body sat firm in position, with my eyes now drilling a hole in the kitchen floor. My mother's stare was deep and I was afraid she would soon discover my true identity.

"Just give me time, I'll figure it out," she said, watching me closely. "If I didn't know any better, I would think that this was one of your little tricks, switching places with Gwen so that she could cover your tracks. But she won't do that for you anymore. Not after your little rendezvous with Sparks."

Again, I was at a loss for information.

She backed away. "I don't want you hanging around him." Then she frowned and shook her head. "But what does it matter—you don't listen to me anyway. Why do I even bother with you?"

Wow, that seemed a little harsh. There was no empathy in her voice whatsoever; she sounded robotic. But that wasn't the only thing that had changed. Looking her over, I noticed how bland she appeared. She was dressed all in gray, with no hint of colour inside or out. Even her green eyes looked like they had been bled dry. That was definitely something I hadn't expected to see. Her spirit was naturally full of colour—was *I* the one responsible for draining it? It saddened me to see her like this.

My train of thought was momentarily distracted when I heard someone else enter the kitchen from behind me. "Mom—Scar and I haven't switched places since we were fifteen," she said, walking towards the sink with an empty plate. Setting the dish down, she turned to me and scowled. "You're on your own this time. You got yourself into this mess, you can get yoursel out of it. I tried to help but you didn't want me to bud in."

Ouch, I thought. Gwen didn't seem to like me at all right now. I didn' blame her though—I heard what Black Scarlett had said to her earlier.

I sat quietly at the kitchen table staring up at the eyes that judged me There they stood, Nancy Drew *and* her mother.

I had to say something, if only to hear the reality of my own voice again. "Gwen—you look nice today."

Well, she didn't like that at all. Apparently she thought I was being insincere.

"Okay, did you hit your head? First you tell me to disappear, and now you're telling me that I look nice? Are you bipolar or something?" she said, walking away.

Keeping my cool demeanour, I thought about how the conversation was taking a nosedive—right into the deep end of hell. Was there no way for me to salvage it? And then a thought occurred to me: they didn't know me anymore. Perhaps if I were to open up and give them a little bit of what they wanted, maybe that would help.

I stood to block the entrance before Gwen could leave. "Wait, Gweny . . ."

"Gweny? Did you just call me Gweny?"

"Um, yes . . ." I answered.

She pushed me aside and exited the room. "Don't call me that."

I sat back down in the chair and shook my head. Her actions had slain me and now I was frightened that whatever I had done in the past was irreconcilable in the future.

My mother turned and opened the oven door. I recognized the smell at once. "Is that meatloaf?"

"Yes," she said. "It's your grandmother's recipe. But don't worry, dear, I know how much you don't like it. We'll give the recipe to someone who *does* appreciate family tradition."

Her words sliced right through my heart. I could feel the tears welling up in my eyes. I had to get out of the kitchen. "I'm sorry you hate me so much!" I cried. My legs burst out of the chair as I ran up the stairs to my room.

Slamming the door, I shuddered. *Everyone here hates me.*

Just then, I heard my mother's voice on the other side of the door. "Scarlett, can I come in?"

There was a moment of disillusion on my part when it seemed as though I was given a bit of reprieve from this angry little world. Did she still care about me?

"Yeah," I said, sitting on the bed.

"Scarlett—I'm sorry," she said, softly. I watched as she opened the door and entered the room. Her look was tender, her eyes apologetic. "I'm just trying to figure out who you are. Do *you* even know anymore?"

What a loaded question, I thought.

She crossed the floor and sat next to me on the bed.

"You hate me, don't you?" I said, looking away.

"No, Scarlett—please don't think that. I could never hate you."

"I'm just awful to everyone—I was hoping you would tell me why."

She let out a deep sigh. "I can't tell you why, honey. You don't always talk to us. If anyone has the answer to that—it would be you."

"But how did I get like this?"

"Life can be very hard sometimes, Scarlett. It's not just you. We all have problems to deal with."

"But I *am* the problem, Mom." I said, patting my chest.

She saw my hand and immediately reacted. "Are you okay? What's wrong?"

My answer was natural, I said it without thinking. "It's just this pain that I had earlier." Immediately I covered my mouth as the words slipped out. Damn, I knew better than to tell my mother about my heart problems. She had the trigger response of a barracuda.

"Oh Scarlett," she said, springing into action. "I'll call the doctor."

"NO!" I screamed. It was one of those instant reflex moments. That would be the worst thing in the world right now. "Sorry, I didn't mean to yell like that, Mom. But I'm fine—no doctors, please."

"Okay . . . okay . . . calm down. Just relax—I'll go get you some water."

I took a deep breath. *Whoa, that was close.* I watched as she stood up and walked away.

"Wait, Mom—I'm fine. I don't need any water. I just . . ." So much of me wanted to tell her the truth, right then and there. But as strong as my desire was to reveal myself, I knew the complications and the harm it would cause to anyone who found out.

"What is it, Scarlett?" she said, with her back to me.

"I'm sorry for being a burden," I blurted out.

She turned to face me. "Scarlett, you're not a burden. You're just . . . challenging," she grinned.

That was the first time I saw her smile. Maybe there was hope for me yet.

"I'm just trying to understand you," she said.

"I know . . . me too."

She gave me a funny look.

"What I meant . . . is that I'm just going through some stuff. You know—teen stuff." *Good cover*, I thought.

"I was a teen, too, Scarlett. You know you can always come and talk to me about anything. I know we've struggled as a family but together we can still get through."

"But what about Dad—will he listen too?"

Her eyes closed as she turned her head away from me. I recognized that expression instantly, my parents had worn it many times in the past. Gwen never saw it though—she was always the good sister. No, that look was intended for me. It was cultivated the very day I was born. It proved true with age as I gradually adopted a lack of respect for rules and authority figures. I knew exactly what that look meant—I had said something inappropriate.

"Scarlett, I have to go fix dinner," she said, her voice fragmented. Her tone now reflected a different emotion. It wasn't just disappointment, it was something darker. She was mournful. Once again, I felt the distance grow between us. She then walked out of the room, closing the door behind her.

What just happened? I shook my head in wonder. My mother had become intensely sombre. Where was the joy she naturally exuded? This was a high-spirited woman whose mind was a palette of bright colours. No one could rein her in, I thought. Not even my reckless antics and misguided misdemeanours could break this woman. She would simply scold me and send me on my path of punishment. It was never harsh though, which is probably why I continued to commit such silly violations.

Truth be told, I actually liked getting caught. I enjoyed the attention I received and felt a closer connection to my parents when I was disciplined. I was a weird kid. But even I—the miscreant—couldn't resist my mother's cheerful exuberance.

Now, here she was, saddled with sorrow. Plus, she couldn't get away from me fast enough.

Looking around at the bedroom setting, I sighed. This was still my room, my bed and my door. But a dark cloud now loomed over my heart when I noticed the biggest change of all.

And I knew, without a doubt, that this was no longer my home.

BLUE BEACON

OOT AND PAW, they walked together as Habock led Black Scarlett through the giant Sumacs of Blue Beacon. Although it was December in southern Ontario, the season had been unusually warm. The recent bouts of precipitation had come in the form of rain instead of snow. Leaves were either vaguely green or mildly roasted as they dangled from the trees. Grasses were growing, flowers were still surviving and some bushes were plump with berries. The air was only slightly cool.

It had been a deceivingly mild season.

The sun's light that had led the two travellers to Blue Beacon had crept out of view, leaving them with the shadows of dusk and now nightfall. The sun's disappearance paved the way for Avari's rise.

Black Scarlett looked down at the path that led through the woods. "Boy—it looks pretty wet in there."

"Pavement is one thing—muddy paths are another," Habock said. "Would you mind carrying me, Scarlett? I don't want to get my paws dirty."

She laughed. "You don't mind climbing down the side of a house or walking over wet roads, but a little dirt . . ."

"Stop making fun," he lectured her. "I don't like licking mud off of myself . . . that's disgusting. Now pick me up, please."

"Okay, okay." She leaned over and gently placed him in the crux of her arms. He wiggled until he was comfortable.

"That's much better. Okay . . . we're about ten minutes away from the clearing. Let's keep moving."

"Alright, hold on," she said, as she made her way through the park. The moon's light now shone overhead.

A sharp cracking noise came from behind them as Black Scarlett quickly spun around. "I don't like this, Habock. I don't come here at night anymore."

"Scarlett, there's no need to fear these woods, they are sacred to Avari. She protects anything good that enters them."

"Tell me something, Habock. How did your father find Queen Armandia's son? Did it have something to do with Avari?"

"Actually—yes. She helped my father save the Queen's son. Avari guided him to the baby when he fell into the river. His body sank deep into the realm of darkness but her light helped penetrate the waters which allowed my father to rescue him. She then led them both to the surface—to safety. Since that time, our family has vowed an undying friendship with her."

"That's amazing, Habock. If you had told me that story two years ago, I probably wouldn't have believed you."

"Probably," he smiled up at her.

They continued on down the path. "I think we're getting close, Habock. I can see the clearing up ahead. Has Avari seen the Mirrorwalkers?"

"Yes, she has seen them. But they won't enter Blue Beacon."

"Why not?"

"Because this is sacred ground, protected by Avari. And also, this is the home of the Ivory asps."

"Whoa . . . whoa . . . aren't those snakes poisonous? Isn't that what killed Cleopatra?"

Habock ignored her question. "*Those* are what have been following us, Scarlett; the noises on the path behind us."

She turned to look around. At first her eyes had trouble spotting anything that wasn't green or brown.

"Look carefully," he said. "They're cryptic."

Then something came into view. A long, green feathery branch slithered out from behind a tree and moved towards them.

"I think I see something." She took a step forward.

Instantly, the animal stopped. It disappeared right in front of them.

"Where'd it go?" she said, squinting her eyes.

"Shhh . . ." Habock said. "They're very timid."

Together, they watched as the animal reappeared, its body slowly returning. As it approached, Black Scarlett was surprised to see that its body had become white. "That's cool . . ."

She bent down as Habock climbed up onto her shoulders. At first it seemed that the animal was going to glide away but instead it disappeared right in front of them.

"It's gone again."

"No, Scarlett. Look at the mud on the path."

She soon realized that the animal had not disappeared but rather, changed colour. Its body was now camouflaged with the mud.

"That's amazing. It's okay little guy," she said, trying to coax it into view.

Scale by scale and feather by feather, the reptile reappeared. Its body was now a soft shade of white.

"Wow—it's so small. It's not even the length of a maple leaf. I've never seen one so small, or feathered for that matter. I didn't know there were any."

"Well, these asps only come out at night—when you're not here," he said, peering down from her shoulders. "They were drawn to these woods when Avari came to life."

"Will it bite me if I touch it?"

"No—it senses the good in you, Scarlett. Make it quick, though. We must get through the woods."

Gently, she pressed her fingers against its tiny plush body. The animal did not disappear this time. It allowed the human to touch it.

"Ivory Asps are the watchers of these woods. They see what enters at all times, even during the day. But they reveal themselves only at night," Habock said.

"But if nothing bad can enter the woods, then why would they need to be cryptic?" she said, petting the animal.

"I didn't say that all bad things couldn't enter the woods, I only said that the Mirrorwalkers couldn't. There are many other bad things out there, Scarlett. And for that reason, the Ivory asps must protect themselves. And for those who do threaten them, their bite is poisonous, like you said earlier."

Immediately, she withdrew her hand. "I see."

Habock laughed. "Oh Scarlett, you have nothing to fear." He looked down at the snake and spoke in a foreign tongue. "Isma daffriena Avari."

"What did you say?"

"I said, hello and that we're here to see Avari."

The snake nodded in response. It then turned and lifted itself into the air. With silent beats of its feathers, it passed by them.

"Follow him—he's going to take us to Avari," Habock said, as he wrapped his body around the hood of her coat.

Black Scarlett marvelled at the flying reptile. "It's so beautiful."

"Scarlett—there's still a lot of beauty out there. You just have to be open to it."

She smiled and nodded, then with mindful steps followed the tiny asp through the woods of Blue Beacon.

REFLECTIONS OF ME

I WAS IN utter shock. Across the bedroom was a giant void: Gwen's bed was missing. I couldn't believe it. Where was it? We used to love sharing our room.

Perched on the pillow next to me was my most beloved childhood toy—a stuffed octopus named Squeegee. Gwen had one too, named Zimmer. They were gifts from Mom and Dad, given to us years ago when we were kids. As twins, we found that even our gifts came in two's, until we turned thirteen, that is. Gwen and I loved getting the same gifts. We weren't the kind of twins who wanted separate identities, we were the ones who would have secretly switched places, had our parents fallen under the spell of separation. *The Parent Trap* was our favourite movie.

I reached beside me and grabbed one of Squeegee's tentacles. I brought him close to my chest as I rested my chin on his purple head. For a moment, I thought I was dreaming and that any minute I would wake up to the happy sounds of my sister greeting me.

Instead, I was brought back to reality by a persistent knock at the door.

"Scar—it's me," Gwen said.

I placed Squeegee back on the pillow, so as not to impart my inner behaviour. Any signs of childhood reflections would probably cripple my purpose here. I had to deliver a different personality. Besides, Gwen wasn't buying my nice side.

Promptly, I stood. I thought about my placement in the room and where it would be best represented. I settled on the bedroom window. There, I could send my gloomy gaze adrift. Staring out the window was the perfect way for me to embrace my future self's solemn side. That would do it, I figured.

As I softly scurried across the room, I caught a glimpse of my reflection or rather, lack of one, in the large mirror that stood atop of the make-up dresser.

I stopped in front of the mirror and leaned in to take a closer look. "Oh my God!" My reflection had disappeared. I turned from side to side to see if I was visible in any way.

Just then, the handle turned as Gwen opened the door and entered the room. "Well, I can see that you're feeling better," she smirked.

Stepping back from the mirror, I gasped. "Hi Gweny, I mean Gwen. What are you doing in here?"

"Well, this used to be my room, too, before you took all of it. Anyway, Mom wanted me to check in on you. I can see that you're feeling better."

"I was just seeing if my face was . . . you know . . . normal," I said, moving away from my non-existent image.

"You can cut it out now, Scar. Your theatrics don't work on me," she said, turning away.

"Wait, Gwen. Why won't you talk to me?"

"Why? What good would that do? You'd just tell me to stay out of your life again. You know, I'm only trying to help you."

"I know that now. Look, we obviously haven't talked for a while, and I think we should."

"I don't have time for this, Scar. I've got to go." With that she walked out into the hallway.

I ran out in front of her. "Then why don't you make some time. I want to talk to you, can't you see that? I'm not being devious or deceitful. I'm being honest. I just want to talk."

"You want to talk to me? Fine. Meet me in my room in five. This better not be a trick."

I smiled. "Great! But wait a minute—where's your room?" I looked away in sheer terror. Again, my mouth was in the lead as my poor brain scrambled to catch up.

Gwen looked at me inquisitively. "Where's *my* room? I thought the problem was your heart not your head."

"I'm . . . I'm not feeling like myself right now. I'm sorry," I said, desperately trying to cover my tracks.

"It's down the hall and on the left. For Pete's sake, Scar—it's not like I moved out of the house," she said, walking away.

I watched as she left. *What is wrong with me?* I stepped back into the bedroom and slowly slinked over to the mirror. Staring at the frame, I couldn't believe what wasn't there. What did it mean? Habock would have the answer. Is this what he meant about knowing too much about the future? I would get heart pains and have no reflection? Perhaps it meant that there could only be one reflection at a time, for only one Scarlett.

Looking down at my wristwatch I realized that it was getting late. *Where was Habock?* I wondered. Perhaps he had returned when I was in the kitchen with Mom. I decided to check the attic first before going to Gwen's room.

In my mind, it was now clear. If I was to stay in this house while he was gone, then I was going to make an attempt at fixing the relationships my future self had with my family. I had to—I pretty much screwed everything else up so far. Besides, what other damage could I do?

If I was going to stay here, then I was going to make some changes. That was the plan.

INTO YOUR HEART, I CALL

LTHOUGH BLACK SCARLETT'S exterior frame resembled that of strength and poise, her heart she believed, had become quite cavernous and empty. Her life had in many ways, shut down. She'd been converted into someone else, by those who sought out to change her future. She had become part of a group that accentuated fear and minimized the natural human tendencies towards peace and kindness. On an invisible leash is how the Mirrorwalkers kept her. That was a secret of course, until a newcomer had unveiled it.

But hope had entered Black Scarlett's life. First, a young man had befriended her and agreed to help rid the world of this evil, and now, another had come to her aid: a small but brave, fearless guide. And with him, he brought a very large friend.

Black Scarlett stood, eyes wide with desire, looking up at the light that beamed down upon her. She felt Habock's kindness beside her and the warm, gentle touch from the moon above. Both were loving, both were genuine. Avari's light was honest; Scarlett felt it penetrating her mind. Images were coming into view: family Christmases, late night giggles with a sister, a father's hug and a mother's smile.

A strange array of emotions stirred inside of her. For a moment, the pains she carried were lifted.

"Hello Scarlett," the tender voice spoke.

Black Scarlett had heard it before, but not for some time. She didn't respond. All she wanted to do was listen.

"Scarlett believes that you have forsaken her. Her heart has been scorn," Habock said, looking up at the light.

The voice was soft and caring. "This I know, but my dear I have not abandoned you. You have trusted those who have deserted kindness, and in doing this you have forsaken yourself."

Black Scarlett let out a breath of sadness.

Cushioned in the sky above her, reaching deep into her soul, was Avari. Her monstrous beauty, her circular light and the devastating glow from her smile were piercing Black Scarlett's deepest fears.

"Speak, my dear. I know it has been some time since we last met," Avari said, understanding the source of her anguish.

"Have you been watching me?"

"Yes. I have been with you all along—even in your darkest moments."

"Then you know why I haven't come. I gave up on hope. It was the day the world stopped for me."

Habock nodded, his eyes filled with empathy. "It's okay. Your loss is paramount. It would be for anyone."

He and Avari watched as the tears dripped down her youthful cheeks.

"Talk to me, Scarlett. I am here for you," Avari said.

"Why can't I change history—why can't I change time?"

Avari looked upon her. "You can. The Mirrorwalkers removed many things from your mind, hope was one of them. And the ticking of time has saddened you, especially with the arrival of this night. But it is only the circumstances that have changed who you are. Deep inside, you are still strong."

"Strong enough to defeat them?"

"Yes. You were made to believe that you could be controlled because they took advantage of your mind. Your anger stemmed from your grief and they seized the moment. It is now time for you to take back your life, Scarlett."

"But will I get my family back?"

"That is up to you my dear. But I will tell you this—the Mirrorwalkers have fed upon your weakened state. If you take away their source of power, then you take away their footing."

Habock nodded in agreement.

"They plan to enter Velvet Elm tonight. If that happens . . ." Black Scarlett said.

Avari stopped her. "You must not let them take Velvet Elm. You know what will happen to all of us. The Spider moon is almost here, which means that they will soon head for the Elms. You must stop them from harnessing Arachne's power. My fate is tied to yours, Scarlett. I fear the future as well for my existence is also in jeopardy."

"I've asked for help, to change the past."

"There *is* another way, and here it is: you must find the Star of Hope and take it to the oldest tree inside Velvet Elm."

"The Tree of Life . . ."

"Yes. There, you must climb the tree and place the Star inside the golden web. You know the web of which I speak. Habock will lead you there. Only then will the powers of the forests be reclaimed for good. The Mirrorwalkers will then retreat to their Leader's grave. They will need time to regain their strength as they search for another path to Arachne. That is when you should strike—when they are inside the cave.

"Your final path will then bring you to the mirrors. They too, are hidden inside the cave. Scarlett—you must destroy them. That is the only way to save what is good and defeat those who desire them. We must put an end to all of this," Avari finished.

"Where is the Star of Hope?" Black Scarlett asked.

Avari smiled down at her. "The Star is hidden in a place where only you will find it. When the time is right, you will know."

She looked into the gentle eyes of the moon. "But how will I know . . ."

"Trust me, Scarlett, you will know. But be careful—there is one who can take the Star from you once it has been found."

"The Leader . . ."

"Yes. After you find it, move swiftly. You will surely be followed. Evil will stop at nothing to destroy the Star."

"We can't do this without a third," Black Scarlett said, her doubt returning.

"That is right." Avari's words were subtle. "There is another who can help you; a mirror image of your own. 'One of strength to bind—two identical of power'."

She recognized the words of the prophecy. "To form the Triangle of Might."

"Yes."

Understanding its meaning, Black Scarlett shook her head. "Gwen will never help me. She doesn't know of the cross I bear. And I don't want her to know—I'd rather have her hate me."

"Scarlett, you must not think that."

"There is someone else . . ." Habock suggested.

Black Scarlett was surprised by his statement. "Someone . . . *who?*"

Before he could say anything, he froze. His senses were distracted. He lifted his nose and sniffed the air. "Do you smell that?" He took a few steps forward.

"It smells like . . . something's burning," Black Scarlett said.

"No—it's just as I feared!" Habock was in shock. His gaze was intense as he watched the flames ignite within the forest ahead of them. "Avari! Behind you! Blazenridge—it's been lit!"

Avari's face turned from them as her light beamed towards the woods across the clearing. "NO! The Leader!"

Black Scarlett looked off into the distance. Her eyes were filled with confusion as red and orange flames now danced around the perimeter of the woods.

Avari turned back, her face filled with horror. "The mirror has been found! The time has come, my dear Habock. You know what needs to be done. Move with haste!"

"We must leave now, Scarlett!" Habock said, jumping onto her shoulders. "NOW!"

As fear and anxiety began to overtake her, she looked back at Avari. "It can't be!"

"Scarlett—be strong. The quest to save the future begins now!"

"But they have the mirror, the one in the attic!"

Avari's eyes were sullen. "Yes—the cobra has found it. Your only choice now is to go to Velvet Elm. Go—my light will guide you!"

Black Scarlett was focused on Avari's words. She had never seen fear in the moon before. Although it frightened her, she relished the notion that her inner strength could prevail over her weaknesses. As a wayward teen, she needed to hear that.

Avari made it clear that Scarlett was needed to save the day; the gavel of justice was within her reach. A surge of hope sprung along her spine. "I won't let you down," she said with conviction.

With those words, Habock began to tremble. "Oh no! The attic—first we must get to the attic!"

"But Habock, there's no time!" Black Scarlett yelled.

"You don't understand—there's something in the attic! We have to go back! Avari—can you stall them?"

For a moment, she was silent. Then her words formed with determination. "I will start an eclipse. My light will disappear for a short time—they will not be able to see. Hopefully that will give you the time you need. Be careful, both of you. And hurry—the celestial alignment begins soon!"

Black Scarlett turned and made her way back into the woods. She watched as the Ivory Asp reappeared, floating in the air in front of her. Habock motioned with his paw the direction in which they were headed. He then spoke in a foreign tongue as the feathered snake bowed its head and began to fly.

Quickly, it skated past the trees as it led them to the other side of the park.

"Scarlett, run—we must get back to the house!"

"Hold on tight, Habock!" she said.

Her feet moved swiftly over the ground as Avari's light glistened behind the trees. The smell of burning wood surrounded Black Scarlett's senses, now filling her body with adrenalin.

Blazenridge forest was lit, which meant that the Leader now controlled the elements of the woods.

Soon, he would be marching to Velvet Elm to claim his victory.

GONE!

Y BODY QUIVERED in place as I looked around the attic. I couldn't believe it—the mirror was gone.

I ran across the floor, moving the boxes that stood in my way. "It can't be gone—it just can't be!" I searched every corner of the room, exasperated. The mirror wasn't there. All that was left was the burgundy fabric that once covered it.

My heart jumped when a voice appeared behind me. "Scar—I thought you wanted to talk. Why are you up here again?" Gwen said, her head poking through the opening in the floor.

"Um . . . Gwen . . . I . . ."

"Just finish what you're doing—I've got to leave soon," she said, her words trailing down the ladder.

I ran over to the window in the hopes of seeing Habock somewhere nearby. Looking through the darkness, I saw only the backyard tree and the red shiny tint of Odin's doghouse. There was no sign of Habock or my future self.

I wondered if they had come back and taken the mirror while I was downstairs. But that didn't seem realistic; it was too big to remove. Besides, Habock would have looked for me first. He knew that I couldn't leave this time without it—it was my only way back to the past. Then I remembered what he said about the Scarlett King Cobra and how it was looking for the mirror. "The cobra must have found it! But how—it was cloaked?" I had no answers for myself. "Great, just great! What am I supposed to do now?"

It was a lost cause. The mirror was gone. Habock and Black Scarlett weren't here—who knows what had happened to them.

I could feel my pulse picking up speed; I was beginning to panic. "Breathe, Scarlett. Breathe." I took a few moments to relax my nerves and although they settled, I knew they would start racing again at any time. I had to keep calm. "Keep your cool," I told myself. "I don't know how, but you're going to fix this."

I walked towards the attic door and stepped down onto the ladder. "Habock, where are you?" I took one last look around, then quietly descended.

As my feet rested on the floor, I heard a noise behind me. When I turned around, I saw the sweet eyes of our German shepherd. His tongue dangled from his mouth as his tail danced behind him. Finally—someone was happy to see me.

Instantly, he began to smell my clothes.

"Oh, it's so good to see you, Odin. How's my buddy doing?" I said, reaching out to pet him. But as soon as he saw my hand, he began to bark.

"It's okay, Odin." I hoped that no one would pick up on his odd response.

His barking quickly evolved into growls and for the first time ever, I saw how fierce his teeth were. He started snapping at me as if I were an intruder.

"Odin—it's me, Scarlett!" I said, trying to silence him. It didn't work and I felt like he was going to attack me.

Just then, my mother ran up the stairs. Gwen darted down the hallway at the same time. They met in the middle and grabbed Odin by the collar as I hid on the other side of the ladder.

"Odin—stop it! It's Scarlett, what's wrong with you?" my mother shrieked. His barking ceased immediately at the sound of her voice.

Both Gwen and my mother looked at me as I stood shaking behind the metal stairs. "Are you okay, dear?" my mother asked.

"I'm fine, just a little rattled. I don't know why he was acting like that," I said, pretending not to know. When I looked over at my sister, she had this strange expression on her face as if she knew something wasn't right.

I tried to diffuse the situation. "I was just on my way to talk to Gwen . . ."

"It's okay, Scarlett. I'm just glad that you're all right. Do you want me to bring you something?" my mother asked.

"No, I'm fine." When I looked back at Gwen, she was gone. "Mom—I've got to go talk to Gwen. Sorry about Odin, I don't know what got into him."

"Well, he's fine now. Odin—what a silly boy you are," she said, petting his head.

He watched me like a hawk as I walked away. I now knew that the cat could talk but I was praying to God that the dog couldn't.

My mother then led Odin down the stairs to the kitchen where I heard his dish fill with kibble. I could hear her voice calmly consoling him.

As I trekked down the hallway to Gwen's room, I thought that I heard someone calling my name. I stopped for a moment and listened. I thought it was my father calling me.

I took a few steps back and leaned over the banister. "Dad—is that you?" I called out. But there was no answer. Patiently I waited, hoping to hear his voice. I hadn't seen him yet in this future time and I was starting to wonder why.

All I heard now was music from the room down the hallway. It was coming from my father's old work room—the one he'd spent hours in, designing commercial campaigns for his advertising firm. *That's weird.* I thought. *Why would Gwen move into that room?*

I continued on, thinking only about the present and where exactly that was going to take me.

PAINFUL DISCOVERY

LTHOUGH THE CONVERSATION started out casual, with me trying to avoid confrontation, it soon turned into my persecution.

"That's the second time you were up in the attic," Gwen said. Her voice was filled with disbelief. "What were you doing up there? You never go up there."

This time, I thought about my answer before speaking. "I went up there because I was feeling melancholy. I wanted to look at our old stuff. I didn't realize that I needed your permission to do that." My response was curt but I figured that if I was stepping into the shoes of my future self, then I better fit them.

"Like you'd ever feel sad over that," she said.

"Look, Gwen. Just so you know, I do in fact have feelings, and sadness happens to be one of them. I feel sad all the time but I bet you never noticed since all you do is judge me."

"Judge you? Are you kidding? I'm the most understanding one here, especially now that our dog doesn't seem to recognize you. Do you mind trying to explain that?" she said, her arms crossed.

"Look, Gwen—I don't know what you're getting at and I don't like your tone."

She pivoted towards the door. "That's it . . . I'm out of here. I've got plans tonight and I don't have time for another fight." She turned the doorknob but then stopped.

"You're just gonna walk away from me . . . is that it? That's all you do nowadays. Why can't you just face me and tell me what's really bothering you?"

She looked back at me with a curious expression.

"What?" I said, defensively.

"Did you hear that?" she said, listening at the door.

"Hear what?"

She pointed to the ceiling. "That! Did you hear it?"

I heard it all right, something was in the attic. I listened closely to the noises above us when I realized what they were—footsteps. I was hoping that it was Habock and Black Scarlett, and no one else. I had to cover for them. "I don't hear anything. Maybe it was the wind."

Gwen rolled her eyes. "It's not the wind, dodo. I heard footsteps in the attic. Someone's up there. And Mom's downstairs."

She was just about to step into the hallway when I blurted out the only answer I could think of, so to stop her from leaving. "It must be Dad, then."

With that, Gwen's whole demeanour changed. She halted all movement and stood quietly at the door. Turning back, she looked at me with fire in her eyes. "What did you say?"

I shook my head. "I said maybe it was Dad." I didn't know where she was headed with this line of questioning and I didn't care because frankly, she looked deranged.

"You think that's funny? Are you crazy?"

"Me crazy? No, but you're acting a little bizarre. Look, if it's not Mom, and you and I are both here, then it stands to reason . . ."

She cut me off mid-sentence. "What's wrong with you Scar? Why would you say something like that?"

I could see the tears building up in her eyes.

Why was she acting like this? I didn't like the vibe I was getting from her. "What aren't you telling me?"

The look she gave me was dismal. "You need to let him go, Scar. Thinking that he's here—it's not helping you to move on. You have to accept it, he's not coming back."

I folded my arms and fought back the onset of tears. "Why can't I hold on?"

"Scar—it's been two-and-a-half years since the accident. You've got to stop blaming yourself. It's not helping anything."

I then knew the source of her bitterness. Something I had done in the past had resulted in my father's death. Gwen blamed me and so did my mother. It was all starting to fall into place: the anger, the revolt, the loss of control and the struggle for peace within this family. These were issues within our house, ones that were avoided because I had delved into the dark side of my heart.

Neither one of us said anything else.

I had to get out of the room. I felt like the air had been sucked from my lungs, collapsing them. My only desire now was to leave this place.

The footsteps had disappeared from the attic, leaving the house silent and painfully still.

Avoiding Gwen's stare, I left the room and made my way down the hallway. As I reached the top of the stairs, I placed my hand on the banister to sturdy myself. And there, in between the walls and the wooden rail, I lowered my head and cried.

DISAPPEARING SECRETS

 ITH CAREFUL STEPS, Black Scarlett climbed down the trellis into the backyard. "I can't believe that the mirror is really gone!"

Habock said nothing. His mind was busy with other matters. Impatiently, he paced back and forth on the grass as he waited for her.

As her feet touched the ground, she repositioned her coat. "I grabbed the map, my backpack and a few other things," she said, tapping the sack on her shoulder. "I think we have everything we need."

Habock looked up at the darkened moon. "We have to get moving—we don't have a lot of time."

Black Scarlett peered up at the sky. "Avari started an eclipse for us—that's amazing."

"She's not supposed to, Scarlett. It plays with the natural order of things. She won't be dark for long, though. If anything, it will only slow the enemy down. I believe there is something very different about this Leader."

"Different—how?"

Habock's small figure skimmed over the grass as he pondered. "I think that he might have chosen a form of possession."

"What do you mean?"

Habock didn't want to reveal too much. He knew that if Scarlett knew the truth, it would hurt her chances of succeeding in bringing this other world to an end. And like her, he wanted life returned to its original state, before the timeline went askew. Habock was fully aware of how Scarlett's life was derailed in the past, but she wasn't the only one affected.

He had arrived on this day for a reason. It was the day of the Leader's ascension and also the day Scarlett was summoned to duty to defeat his family's Kingdom. Her sole purpose as a soldier was to retrieve the mirror. But without a mirror to find, Scarlett would not be sent there and the Leader would be at a loss.

Habock knew that by bringing Sparks into the story, Scarlett would then have an ally; someone strong to pull her away from evil.

Scarlett, unaware with what was about to happen, prepared the diary for time travel. In it, she warned her past self about a tragic event that would take place. All she needed was a way to get it there—Habock was the key.

Little did she know that they had met before and that her memories of him were erased by the Mirrorwalkers. They had tried everything in their power to keep Scarlett blind to his true existence but they had slipped. She had overheard them one night talking about Habock, and how he would arrive in the future one day to find her. A mysterious figure had contacted the Mirrorwalkers and instructed them to prepare for Habock's arrival.

But the smart little feline had secrets of his own; one of which was burned inside his mind. It involved stolen power and a body that was taken.

During the fall of the three Kingdoms, Scarlett had become one the Mirrorwalkers' most powerful warriors. Habock didn't understand why she'd been chosen, so when the time came for him to leave his home, he and his family decided that she would be the bearer of the mirror. He believed that he could keep her out of harm's way, if only he was there to protect her. Evil yearned for Scarlett, so Habock concluded that he would devote all of his time to guiding her down the path of good.

Back in time he travelled, making a few stops along the way to see where Scarlett had been corrupted. He took the diary with him on one of his stops. Then even further back he went to a time of complete innocence, just after she was born.

Habock landed in the attic when Scarlett was only three months old. He was surprised to learn that she had a twin sister. He hadn't seen Gwen on any of his stops to the past. And it was something that he never forgot.

After arriving in the attic, Habock meowed mercilessly to be released from the room. Scarlett's mother had discovered him pawing at the ceiling door. His arrival was well received as even she couldn't resist his magnetic charm. Within hours, Habock was adopted into the family. And there he remained, loyally by Scarlett's side. For the next fifteen years, he would act as her guardian angel.

Years went by and the sisters grew.

Gwen, as it turned out, was the good daughter; the one who didn't need any counsel or guidance. Scarlett however, was the cause of many worry lines and grief.

Although Habock found her reckless behaviour somewhat challenging at times, he was there regardless, to intercept any chance meetings she had with the Mirrorwalkers. He was determined to foil their attempts at manipulating her.

Ironically, Scarlett had no sense of timing. This unforeseen trait, humoured Habock greatly. His amusement faded though as a certain date slowly approached. Habock knew that as Scarlett's sixteenth birthday marched towards her, so did the Mirrorwalkers.

He remembered one of the stops he had taken en route to Scarlett's attic. It was the point at which her life was thrown into upheaval. It was also the time that the Mirrorwalkers first recruited her. Habock wanted to know how this was accomplished.

Then he found out about her father's death. Tragedy, as it were, had led Scarlett down the path of evil. And now he discovered that that event had occurred once again. Whether he was a part of her life or not, Habock now understood that he was unable to stop her father's death.

The masks of the enemy surrounded his thoughts as he drifted over the sea of grass. One face stood out amongst the mass of evil monsters. And in his heart he knew, that when he had travelled to the past fifteen years ago—he wasn't alone.

Habock gazed up at the attic window. He shook his head, fearing the inevitable.

"Are you okay?" Black Scarlett said. "You look a little frazzled."

"I'm just anxious. I think something else was taken."

"Like what?"

"I can't say."

"Well then, let's go, Habock. We've got to get to the forest."

He responded with a nod. His black-tipped body turned and propelled across the yard as he headed for the street. Habock was designed for speed his feet nimble and spirited.

Black Scarlett followed behind closely as she watched his tail wag back and forth ahead of her.

He glanced back. "You okay?"

"I'm fine." She stared at his black furry face, his sapphire eyes glowing in the night. His vision was leading the way. "Habock—are you sure this is going to work?"

"I have to believe that it will," he said, looking back at the street.

"I brought a flashlight."

"We don't need it. You've got me."

"Okay, I'm behind you one hundred percent, Habock. I believe we can do this."

Neither one of them knew what to expect, yet both were determined to fight on the side of hope. Habock had reminded Black Scarlett of her place in the world and the goodness she was capable of achieving. Avari had reinforced it.

Their only hope now was that they could get there in time.

BLAZENRIDGE FOREST

VELVET ELM

TAMS

FINLAKE FIR FOREST

GRINSTONE GAIL FOREST

FAIRY TALES

EARS STREAMED DOWN my face with all the emotions of the day racing after them. Here I was, stranded in a strange time without my guide, without the mirror and now without my father. There was no reason for me to be here, I had learned all that I needed to know. I saw what happened to my family after some accident in the past claimed my father's life. All I wanted to do was go back in time and stop that from happening.

What I needed was a way to get there.

Standing in the middle of the stairs, I looked around. It sounded like my mother was in the basement doing laundry and Gwen was still in her room, getting ready to leave. Odin was in the kitchen drinking—I could hear him lapping up the water in his dish. I didn't want to arouse any more suspicion, so I tiptoed down the remaining stairs and headed for the front door. I grabbed a coat off of the hook by the door and quickly exited the house.

As I closed the door behind me, it dawned on me that this was still my neighbourhood—I wasn't really lost. The diary talked about the triangle of forests with Velvet Elm in the centre; all of which were in walking distance from my house. I knew where all of those places were, and so through the darkness I walked, with the black stone and Uncle Frankie's letter in my pocket.

This was good, I had a starting point. Better yet, I knew my way around in the dark—it was usually the time I arrived home, after curfew.

It did seem oddly dark though, considering it was supposed to be a full moon tonight. I looked up at the sky and saw a shadow over the moon "There's an eclipse tonight? Wow!" I stared at the sky in awe of the night's event. But in spite of my outward fascination, my heart remained gloomy. What was the point of seeing anything good here? This was no longer my world.

Continuing on, I thought about the stone in my pocket. I could feel it now, rubbing against my leg in the envelope. Although I hadn't read Uncle Frankie's letter, I had a sneaking suspicion that I knew what it was about. I figured that at some point in the past, Habock had introduced himself to Frankie—verbally.

I wanted to read the letter but now was not the time.

The diary said something about Blazenridge being taken and then some inaccuracy about the rise of the Leader—whatever that meant. So, I took a stab at figuring things out for myself.

My brain focussed on the three forests discussed in the diary: Finlake Fir, Grinstone Gail and Blazenridge. Each housed a momentous assortment of trees. From the towering Tulips to the monster Sequoia's, each one was littered with arboreal giants. Scattered Maples brightened the woods with colour while the Pines and Tamaracks added points and cones. As a working conglomerate, the woods thrived throughout the seasons. Each came alive and then fell silent during the revolution of the year.

As I walked down the road, I tried to remember the old fairy tale about the forests. Although they existed, the fairy tale did not—or at least that's what I thought. Together, they formed a triangle around Velvet Elm—an ancient forest filled entirely with archaic Elm trees.

It was said that Velvet Elm was where the colours of the Earth came together and the animals danced freely. It was a child's fairy tale told in the spirit of magic. No one really believed it. But then I came here, to this time, and things started to change for me. Maybe there *was* some truth to it.

I heard the story when I was young—Gwen and I were just kids. My father told us that the three woods in the triangle reflected three elements on Earth; Finlake Fir was water, Grinstone Gail was air, Blazenridge was fire. It was said that Blazenridge was the hardest forest of the three to harness, which made it the pinnacle of challenge. In the hands of good, the forests would remain at peace but in the hands of evil they would be dangerous to enter. And if Blazenridge was set afire, it was due to the evil forces that seized it. Then nothing could stop them from capturing Velvet Elm. That was the story.

We always thought that our father made the whole thing up—it was just too silly to be real.

Now, all those nights of story-time tales came flooding back to me. I could hear my father's voice. I could see the twinkle in his eyes. He lit up every time he told it.

I looked back and saw the house getting smaller behind me. I was on a mission to find Habock and get out of this place. Nothing was going to stop me.

*　　*　　*

The light from the attic now poured out into the backyard and onto the road that passed by it.

Behind the glass window stood a dark shadow looking out. It watched as Scarlett disappeared down the street.

Its eyes were silvery and mystic, and it wore a devilish grin. The figure then turned from the window to face the velvet fabric on the floor. It closed the diary in its hands and spoke with a sharp tongue. "Want to go home, do you? We'll just see about that!"

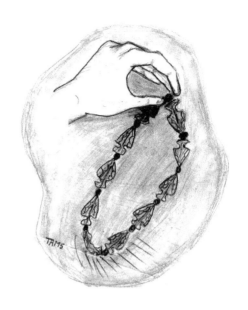

FORGOTTEN MEETING

"ABOCK—WAIT!" BLACK SCARLETT said, stopping on the road.

"What is it?" he said.

"It's Sparks. I totally forgot—I was supposed to meet with him tonight! Damn! He's gonna think I abandoned him. I've got to let him know." She reached into her backpack and fumbled with her fingers. "Shoot—I don't have my cell phone. Mom took it because I was grounded. How am I supposed to get a hold of him?" She paused. "I've got to go back."

Habock tried to stop her. "Wait—where were you supposed to meet?" His words trailed behind her as she ran down the road in the direction they had just come from. "Scarlett—come back!" he hollered.

A moment later his voice caught up with her. She was standing in the middle of the street.

He walked up alongside her. "You won't get far in this."

The area in front of them was now coated in a blanket of thick fog. Neither one of them could see.

Black Scarlett was completely stunned. "Where did this come from? We just came from here!"

"It would appear that someone does not want us to go back. And we can't go back—even I can't see in there," he said, peering through the haze.

"Habock—what am I gonna do? He's waiting for me."

"Scarlett, listen to me. We have to keep going. Avari can only hold the Mirrorwalkers off for so long. Sparks will understand."

"But he doesn't know what's happened, and I need him."

"No, Scarlett—you don't. I'm here."

"You don't understand, Habock . . ."

He interrupted her words with force. "Scarlett—you're being selfish! I've lost a lot coming here. It's not just about *you* anymore—do you understand? There are other things at stake!"

Black Scarlett didn't respond.

"I'm sorry, Scarlett. It's just that you don't know what I've risked to come here. I've lost some things, too. And I can't tell you all I know because it will change things, so please don't ask. Just help me do what needs to be done. We will do it together."

"I'm sorry, Habock. I didn't mean to upset you. You're right—Sparks will understand. Are you okay?"

He nodded. "I will be when this is all done."

"Are we cool?" she asked.

He looked up at her and smiled. "Yes, we're cool. Look—I'm sorry I yelled. It's just that we need to move on. Time is slipping away from us."

"Okay then, I'm ready to go. So, who do you think is behind all this fog?"

"There's only one I can think of . . ." There was a lull in his voice. "Wait just a minute."

"What is it?"

Habock squinted. "Take off your coat."

"What? Are you crazy? It's cold out here," she said, folding her arms.

He winked at her. "It's just for a moment." He then placed his paw over his mouth.

Black Scarlett obliged. She unzipped the coat and removed it.

Habock jumped onto her shoulders and grabbed the necklace between his teeth. He cut through the string that held the jewels together, and with one sharp bite, they fell to the ground.

"What are you doing?" As she reached down to pick it up, Habock jumped to the ground and dragged the necklace away from her. He shook his head indicating that she was to leave it. Using his teeth, he threw it into the fog.

"What did you do that for?" she mouthed. "That was a gift!"

"Leave it, Scarlett. I'll explain later. Put your coat on and let's go," he said, quietly.

Although she resisted at first, she eventually picked up the coat and followed behind Habock. Looking back, she pulled up the zipper and frowned.

They walked without words as they continued on the path towards the forests. Habock carried yet another secret. But this one, he believed, would prove to be promising.

AND THEN THERE WERE TWO

WAS HEADED for the woodland triumvirate. Although the area was dark around me, I knew my way quite well. I simply followed my feet—they knew where they were going.

Although the light from the moon was hidden by the eclipse, I could feel the power behind it. I wondered if I would get the chance to talk to Avari before I returned home, although the idea still sounded somewhat ludicrous.

Just as I was losing my train of thought, I heard a noise up ahead of me on the road.

Immediately, I stopped to listen. It appeared that the sound was moving away. "Hello?" I no longer cared about being exposed. I waited for a response but none came.

I noticed that the area was now cloudy; the road was obscured from view. "Great—now what?" Taking a few steps, I stretched out my hands in front of me. I could barely see them. Although I was adept at moving around in the darkness, I was blinded by the haze that was creeping in. "Where did that come from? What is going on around here?" Something deep in my skin was telling me to go back, and yet all I wanted to do was continue onward. I had this weird feeling that something was trying to stop me from reaching the forests.

At that very moment, something small flew right in front of me. It brushed over my head as it circled the spot where I was standing. I covered my head with my hands. "What the—"

Looking out between my fingers, I saw a tiny blue neon body hovering over me. Its thin white wings thrust up and down as it moved around me. I had no idea what it was doing. Its little body then lifted up and disappeared into the trees by the side of the road. "What was *that?*"

I stood in the middle of the road, contemplating my next move when something beside me seized my attention. A short pulse of white energy burst through the air. It was like a beacon, flashing in the night. "Now what?" I thought I had stumbled across a family of fireflies but I ruled that out when I remembered what month it was.

Again, I watched as the air ignited with a series of luminescent flashes. "Scar—over here!" a guy's voice called out from behind the bushes on the side of the road. "It's me!"

I peered into the shrubs and saw a figure moving out towards me on the street. He was calling my name. *Oh great, I'm supposed to know who that is?*

Whoever it was, apparently thought I was the future Scarlett. Boy, was he in for a surprise.

"Who's there?" I answered.

"Scar—it's me. Sparks!" he said.

Right. Okay. Sparks. I knew the name but didn't know the face. Just when I thought my acting days were over. Now I had to pretend like I knew who this was. *Great, just great.*

"Sparks? What are you doing here?"

"I was waiting for you. This is where we were supposed to meet, remember?"

"Oh, right," I nodded in forged compliance.

Just as he approached, a flash of light washed over my eyes and I was momentarily stunned. "What is that?"

"That's our secret signal—don't you remember?" He was holding a large flashlight in front of him.

"Wow—that's really bright."

"Yeah—I know. Isn't it great? Wait until you see the red one."

As soon as my vision returned, I saw his face in front of me. "Wait a minute—I know you. You're that boy from school, the one I missed dinner for. You're the reason I was sent to the attic to clean. *You're* Sparks?"

He looked at me with a strange grin. "You okay, Scar? You seem a little disoriented."

Then I remembered what Habock had said about giving this boy a push at school, dangling the bait, that sort of thing. "You're Sparks—of course! Now it's all starting to make sense."

His smile disappeared and a look of concern replaced it. "Did something happen to you?"

A deep-rooted feeling sprouted inside of me and for whatever reason I felt like I couldn't lie to this guy. He seemed utterly innocent. All I wanted to do was desert my oath and reveal my secret identity. "You don't remember me, do you?"

He took a step back. "Gwen—is that you?"

"Not quite," I said. "Tell me, Sparks, are we good friends in the future . . . I mean . . . *now?*"

He seemed reluctant to answer me.

"Okay. I have to tell you something and you have to promise me that you won't freak out. What I'm going to tell you is pretty weird and you might not think it's possible . . ." Now I was rambling. *Get a grip, Scarlett.* "Look, I'm just gonna come out and say it—"

He intercepted my words just as I was about to spill the beans. "You're Scarlett, from the past."

I was astounded by his answer. "How did you know that?"

"Because you look like her, back when I first met you that is. I remember when you used to wear orange Converse. Now you only wear black ones."

"Wow . . . you're pretty observant. Doesn't this freak you out at all?"

He circled around me, looking me over. "Yep—that's you all right. So I guess Scarlett from this time is out there somewhere with a talking cat?" he smiled.

"Whoa, how did you know that?"

Sparks began to pace in front of me. "Scar and I half expected this, at least the cat part. You—I just guessed."

"Well, now things are all fouled up. She's out there with Habock—the cat—heading for Blazenridge or Velvet Elm, I think, and I'm left here . . ."

"Did you say Blazenridge?" His tone was grave. He became very serious at the mere mention of the forest.

"Yes . . . I think that's where they were going. It was that or Velvet Elm. First, they went to see Avari at Blue Beacon, and then I was caught by Gwen in the attic. So I pretended to be Scarlett of this time. I think

Habock and Black Scarlett—that's what I call her—came back to the attic and left again. I didn't see them but I think it was them."

"Gwen saw you?" he said.

"Yes, and when I went back up to the attic, the mirror was gone—the one that brought me here to this time. Now I have no way to get home."

"The mirror is missing?"

"Yeah, I don't know where it is," I said.

"Then that's where they've gone—to the forests." He seemed sure of his answer.

"Good, then can you please tell me what's going on?"

He didn't answer. Instead, he took me behind the bushes where he had stashed a backpack full of papers and other items. "There are a few things that you need to know before you go anywhere."

We knelt down on the ground as he pulled out a map. Unrolling it, he showed me the three forests that surrounded Velvet Elm. Beneath one of them was a secret passage, one that Black Scarlett and Sparks had dug themselves. He had no qualms about disclosing this information.

He showed me the obstacles they had to overcome in order to enter the forests, once they were in the hands of the Mirrorwalkers. Finlake Fir would drown in its own waters. Grinstone Gail would be torn apart by ferocious winds. And Blazenridge would suffer the burning of its own flames.

Sparks and Black Scarlett's plan was incredibly detailed; it was all laid out before me, step by step.

"I can't believe this." I looked up at him with sheer shock in my eyes. I was completely stupefied. "Habock told me things, and I heard other stuff in the diary. But to be honest, I didn't really believe it. It just didn't seem real."

"Oh, it's real, Scarlett. I wish it wasn't."

Nothing seemed legitimate to me, but at that moment it didn't matter. There was a more pressing question that I wanted answered. I felt like Sparks would be the one to ask. After six minutes of conversing with him, I felt a connection to his soul. I could tell that honesty was his greatest attribute.

"What about my father—do you know what happened to him? Did he really die in an accident?"

He paused for a moment. "Yes—it's true. I'm so sorry, Scar. He died the night of your party—the night you turned sixteen."

My eyes began to water. But this time, I decided to be strong. "Tell me what happened, Sparks. I need to know. Did *I* cause the accident?"

I don't think he wanted to tell me what happened but I pushed for an answer, so he gave me one.

"On the night of your party, your dad drove to a restaurant to get pizza for you, Gwen and all your friends. You went with him in the car. Later, you told me that you got into a fight on the way there. When you went over the Harrington Bridge, he swerved to miss a hitchhiker on the road and your car went into the river."

Already, the story was getting too difficult to hear. But I wanted to know the ending so if anything, I could go back in time and prevent it from happening.

"Do you want me to continue?"

"Finish it," I said.

"The car went into the river and sank in the water. You were able to get out unharmed but your dad was knocked unconscious. You told everyone that you got him out of the car and took him to a spot underneath the bridge. But it was too late. He was already gone. We later found out that the blunt force to his head caused severe internal bleeding. You couldn't save him. Scar, I know what you're thinking but there's nothing else you could have done."

I wept in response. "Do you know what we fought about in the car?"

Sparks hesitated. "The fight was about me."

"You? *Why?*"

"Your parents didn't like me, Scar. They didn't want me at your party. The night before, you were out with me. Gwen got caught lying to protect you. She then told your parents about us."

I turned from his voice. "That's not like Gweny at all. She would never rat on me."

Sparks was quiet.

"So, it *was* something that I did. It *was* my fault."

"No, Scar, it wasn't," he said, handing me a tissue from his pocket. "Someone else caused the accident, and that someone was waiting for you on the road that night."

I looked back at him. "Waiting for me?"

"Yes," he said. "Someone who knew you were coming."

I was horrified to hear this. "Who?"

The words trickled from his lips, like blood seeping from a wound. They pierced through my ears as fury grew in my veins. I wasn't too sure who was responsible for provoking this madness inside of me, whether it was Habock, Sparks or myself. But I couldn't let it lie.

I was drawn into this mess for a reason, and I think I had just found out why.

STRENGTH FROM PAIN

WAS ENRAGED. This was without a doubt, the most furious I had ever been in my entire life. My arms were flailing about recklessly and my mouth was uninhibited. Like a noisy kettle ready to blow, I had reached my boiling point.

"How dare you say that! Don't forget who you're talking to buddy!" I spurted.

"I'm not trying to hurt you, Scar. I'm just trying to show you what I think is true," Sparks said.

"Oh, really? Cause right now I think you're insane!" My legs were alive with activity and my mind wouldn't allow them to sit. I was moving back and forth like a madwoman. "How could you even *propose* something like that?"

"Would you please calm down, I would like to talk to you rationally," he said.

I spun around to face him. "How could you say something like that, my own flesh and blood? Did you tell Black Scarlett?"

"No, I was going to tell her tonight. Look, Scar—I'm sorry. I really am. But the pieces all fit, think about it."

"I don't want to think about it! This is all wrong! I don't know where I am anymore but this is *not* the world I know. I must be dreaming because this can't be happening!" I closed my eyes in a last ditch effort to leave this place behind.

For a moment, the darkness put my thoughts at ease. I could hear the words of my father in the back of my head. '*Simmer down, Scarlett,*' he would say. '*Let the world spin around a few times*'. God, I missed his voice.

Gradually, my emotions started to melt. The outrage that flamed inside of me began to dissipate and I could feel my heart starting to settle.

When I opened my eyes, I saw the peaceful sway of the trees. I breathed in the cool air around me. Time seemed to move a little slower.

"You're still here," I heard a voice on the ground. Looking down, I saw Sparks sitting in front of me. "Are you okay?"

My words were sluggish as they dribbled out of my mouth. "It can't be true, Sparks—it just can't be. She's been there my whole life. How could she be this monster that you're talking about?"

"Scar, none of us even imagined it. Gwen fooled us all. *She* was the Leader inside your house and wore a mask that not even you could see through."

"This is just way too much. How did she find out about the mirror—did I let it slip somehow?"

"I don't know."

"Well, what about my sister? Did she turn into this thing or was she ever my sister at all?"

"I'm not sure. I know that things started to change around the time you both turned sixteen."

My denial was now vestigial. "Really?"

Learning all of this was comparable to discovering an ancient prophecy that revealed only bad news. I hated hearing it. And not one part of me wanted to believe it.

"They took you after the night of your party," Sparks said. "I don't know what they did to you, Scar, but you were gone for a while—a little over a year. Your mom thought you ran away."

I looked at him in disbelief. "Oh my God—no wonder she was so depressed. I left her all alone with that monster in the house. Look at what I put her through!"

"But Scar," he continued, "I found you and brought you home. I wasn't going to let them keep you. Gwen must have known that we were in cahoots because she told your mother that I was dangerous to be around. After you came back, we had to sneak around to be together."

"That's why she didn't want me hanging around you. It all makes sense now," I said, understanding the situation. "You and I had something going on."

"Yes, although your parents never liked me from the start. Probably because Gwen told them things; lies to conceal her plan and to keep us apart. She must have known what we were up to. I'm really sorry, Scar. I didn't want to believe it either. But I think it's the truth. The Leader was already here. They knew you were coming because *Gwen* knew you were coming."

"All this time?" I felt as if the world was now watching me.

"Yes, I think so," he said.

Although part of me wanted to stay in the ring a little longer, the rest of me was done wrestling this match. It was time for me to accept the truth. I now understood what Habock was trying to tell me; the story wasn't just about me anymore. It was about family, friends and beings that I had never met.

This fabricated sister of mine was a great source of evil. I remembered how she acted in the house—her new room, pushing me away, making me feel like the adopted child.

Gwen wasn't real. Maybe she never was. There was one thing that I knew for sure though—she was deadly. Some siblings said it without meaning, but mine was actually true.

All the past memories came thundering back to me; family dinners, doctor's visits, breaking curfew through a bedroom window.

"Sparks—I just need a minute," I said, allowing the tears to fall.

He didn't answer. Instead, I felt his arms wrap around me as I lowered my head into his shoulder.

"How could I have not seen it?"

"It's okay, Scar," he said, holding me. "You weren't the only one."

"I'm so stupid."

"No, no you're not. You were deceived—we all were."

"But even Habock tried to . . ." I stopped. "Oh no." Lifting my head, I gazed into his eyes. "Habock!"

"What about him?"

"Don't you see? He's with the other Scarlett right now. Don't they need you, Sparks?"

I could see the effort behind his thoughts. "You said that they went to talk to Avari?"

"Yes, to Blue Beacon. That's where they were headed when I was in the attic."

"Well, Scar and I need a third; the prophecy of three. But if Habock took her to see Avari, then they must have another plan," he said.

"Would they still go to Velvet Elm?"

"Yes, because that's where the Leader was headed. Scar was ready to stop him, no matter what it took. He *will* capture Velvet Elm. That, we know for sure."

"But what about the mirrors—where are they?" I asked.

"They're inside Finlake Forest."

I nodded. "Right, I remember this. Near the Leader's grave, beneath the Silver Flint, right? Tell me Sparks, would you be able to find the cave?"

"I don't know—maybe. I didn't see anything when I was there. I only found Scarlett when she was wandering through the forest."

"How did you know where to find her?" I asked. "I mean, you happened to be there on the very day that she escaped—that's quite the coincidence."

"No, it's not," he said. "I went to that forest every day looking for her."

His answer blew me away. I couldn't believe how amazingly kind this guy was. No wonder I liked him.

"As for the cave," he continued, "finding it will be difficult because it moves."

"Wait a minute—I think I heard Black Scarlett say that in the diary. The Gypsy Sands that move."

"Yeah, except she doesn't remember where any of that is—they did a whammy job on her."

"But I bet Habock could find it . . ." I knew how smart that cat was. He was capable of anything and everything. There was no doubt in my mind that he already had a plan drawn up, ready for action. What that was exactly, I had no idea. But regardless, I had faith in him.

"Maybe, but we have a bigger problem, Scar. If the Leader has found the third mirror, then he's now in control of the three forests. That means Finlake is filled with water. Think of it as a colossal aquarium with an invisible outer shell—it keeps the water in. Everything in there will drown, except for the Gobblinsharks. They'll be protecting it."

"So, if we can help them take back the forests, then we can enter Finlake?"

"Yes," he said.

"Then what?"

"Then the mirrors have to be destroyed."

"That's it? That's all we have to do?"

Sparks applied the brakes to the conversation. "Hold on, hold on. Let's slow down here. There are obstacles, Scar. The Mirrorwalkers, Robberflies . . . ."

"Wait," I interrupted, "are they bright blue and look like small dragonflies? Because I saw one right before I saw you. It flew around me and then took off."

"Yeah, that's them—which probably means that more are coming. They must be watching us."

At that moment, I felt a weird vibe all around me. A surge of power swirled through my body as it climbed the steps of my backbone. I hadn't felt anything quite like it before. Courage and fortitude infiltrated my mind as if a needle filled with liquid valour had been jabbed into my arm. Strength that I had never known now filled my every thought. And like a ship's anchor thrown overboard to prevent drifting, my heart and feet were firmly planted to the ground.

I was unstoppable, unshakable—indifferent to pain. I would not let my emotions, injustices or family ties sweep me away. Female superhero's brimming with power, popped into my head: Catwoman, Black Canary, the Scarlet Witch—

"Whoa . . . did you see that? Your body just lit up!" Sparks said, his voice unsettled.

"It did? Did you see something in front of me?"

"In front of you—how about all around you! You glowed. That was really strange, do you feel okay?"

"Yeah," I laughed. "I feel good. My body feels strong." I stretched out my arms and looked down at my legs.

Sparks examined my new behaviour with scrutiny. "Are you sure you're okay? You're not sick or hurt or something?"

"No—I feel great! Better than that, Sparks, I feel amazing! I don't know what just happened to me but I feel energized—like I could tackle any problem."

"Okay, Scar. That's weird. I think maybe you should sit down."

"Sit down, are you crazy? We've got work to do!"

"Okay—that's the part that scares me. You weren't acting like this a few minutes ago. So, where's this coming from?" His expression was sincere and so was his concern.

"I don't know, Avari maybe?" I guessed.

"Or Gwen—it could be a trap."

"But it's still me in here. I just feel really confident now. And I think I know what needs to be done."

As level headed as he could be, Sparks tried to rationalize with me. But there was no use; I was in a forwardly aggressive state.

My words were spry and spirited. "I think you better get ready for some action." I looked at him with steady eyes. There was no backing down from this feeling, not that I wanted to anyway.

"Sparks," I smiled, "I believe the wheels of change just turned in our favour."

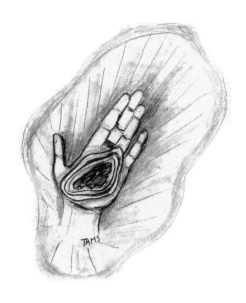

POWER FROM WITHIN

"I DON'T THINK I like this, Scar."

"It's okay, Sparks. Believe me—I feel great!" I walked over and picked up the map. I excused any signs of defeat as my face now assumed a look of enthusiasm. "So, this is where the hidden tunnel is? It's under Grinstone Gail?"

He nodded. "Yes, that's probably where they're headed. Scar wouldn't have gone through the woods—they'd be waiting for her there. Besides, she wouldn't have made it in those winds anyway."

As I pondered my next move, I felt a tiny prick on my leg. Then I remembered what was in my pocket. "Let me ask you something, Sparks. If Gwen knew I was coming, then she would have known about me in the attic right? She probably knew it was me from the past."

"Probably," he said.

"And by saying that, she probably knows where I am right now."

"Most likely. Why? What are you thinking?"

I could tell that he was still preoccupied with my sudden change of dauntlessness. "Well, how does she know that?" I said. "My clothes were different and I wasn't wearing the necklace, but unless she saw the two of us together, she wouldn't know. I mean, my own mother didn't know."

"Seriously? Your mom didn't know?"

"No—she didn't. And I'm surprised because she *always* knew when Gwen and I switched places. But I don't look that different in the future, maybe that's why she didn't know. And what else would she think? For Pete's sake, she didn't have triplets."

Sparks was amused by my comment.

"It's just . . . how would Gwen know?"

He shrugged. "Did Gwen see you go through the mirror to come here?"

"No, Habock and I were alone in the attic. And the mirror was cloaked—only he and I could see it. So how would Gwen know about me?"

"Maybe it was through your psychic connection as a twin," he suggested.

"I think it's something else." From this rollercoaster of recent events, came a new sensation. I had discovered something important on my own and it felt incredible. I believed it would be an important contribution.

Sparks waited patiently for my delivery.

"Her necklace," I grinned. "You know—the jewels around her neck?"

"What about them?"

"I think the necklace is some sort of tracking device, via the stones. Habock told me a little bit about the three Kingdoms and how they used mountain stones to detect when evil had entered their domain. He said that the stones had been stolen and were now in the hands of the Mirrorwalkers. Then, when Habock and I saw Black Scarlett in the attic, she was wearing a necklace with black jewels."

"But how did you know . . ." he started.

"You just told me. You said that Gwen was the Leader, and as much as I don't want to believe it, there are certain parts of my past that fit into this scenario. One of them was a birthday gift from our parents.

When we turned thirteen, I got a diary and Gwen got a bag of stones. I thought it was weird because we used to always get the same gifts."

He nodded as if to understand.

"The diary was beautiful, I remember gloating about it. Gwen showed me her gift briefly, but after that, I never saw the stones again." I pulled the envelope out of my pocket and took out the broken jewel. "I found this in my Uncle Frankie's jacket today. It was in a box with his old clothes, from when he was admitted into the nursing home." Slowly, I uncurled my fingers to reveal the stone.

"Scar didn't tell me much about him; she found it too difficult to talk about," Sparks said, staring at the object in my hand. He then pressed his fingers against his forehead and closed his eyes.

"Yeah, it was difficult. My uncle had a stroke when he was forty-two. It was a devastating blow to my mom because it was her little brother. After he was released from the hospital, we helped take care of him and the nurses came everyday to his apartment to work with him.

"Roughly eight months after his stroke, the doctors raved about his progress. He started coming back over to the house for dinner and acting like his normal self.

Sparks gave an empathizing look as if he knew I was about to say something unpleasant.

"Things were looking up. Then one day he came over to the house and went up to the attic to look for a tennis racket. God, I remember this like it was yesterday. He came down from the attic feeling disoriented and that's when he started talking gibberish. He was spewing weird comments, and later, we found him chasing small animals around the yard. My aunt and sister found him running after a squirrel with a baseball bat."

Sparks' eyes were kind; he seemed to understand my woes. Not one part of him appeared judgemental. *What a nice guy*, I thought.

"We figured that it was some sort of backlash from the stroke. After that, my family took him to Blue Meadows Nursing Home. That's where he's been ever since."

I took a deep breath and sighed. I hadn't told that story to anyone, not even my friends at school. I was extremely sad and embarrassed to talk about it. But it felt good to finally get the words out.

"Scar—he's lucky to have a family that loves him so much."

"Thank you for saying that. Sorry about the tangent, but I wanted to explain that to you. When I was in the attic earlier, I found an old letter that Frankie had written me, and he left this stone with it. I've only skimmed the letter, I haven't read it. But he mentions a talking cat, so at some point he must have spoken to Habock."

"Oh wow," Sparks gasped.

"If Frankie found Gwen's stone in the attic, then I bet that's why he was different afterwards. We all thought it was the stroke, but what if *she* was the cause of his delirium?"

Sparks nodded in agreement. I could tell that he understood my train of thought.

"Chasing after talking animals was what cemented my parent's decision to put him in the home. We took most of the stuff from his apartment and stored it up in the attic. I guess none of us looked through the boxes. Until today, when I put on his jacket and found the stone and the letter in the pocket. I left the attic and then the mirror was taken. Don't you see? Gwen knew it was there because she saw it through the stone I was carrying. This stone is the key!"

"It sounds crazy but I think you might be on to something," Sparks said. "The necklace that Scar wore was a gift from Gwen. She loved it and swore that she would never take it off. Scar, hand me that letter—let's see what your uncle wrote."

I listened as Sparks read each line aloud. Uncle Frankie described several incidents involving animals but only one stood out: the time he met Habock in the attic. Uncle Frankie didn't write much about it but he did say that the conversation revolved around me. He warned me that someday someone would find me, and that I would be in trouble.

The remainder of the letter was devoted to the stone that now rested in my hand. Frankie described it in detail. He said that a curse had been placed upon it by those who needed its power for evil. Although his fear penetrated through the paper, he did not want me to dispose of the stone. Instead, he suggested that I 'use its power to play them'.

I wasn't too sure what he meant by that. The last sentence however, I understood clearly. The words reverberated in my ears. 'Be careful, Scarlett,' it said. 'There's something wrong with Gwen.'

Sparks gazed up at me. "Well, it confirms what we already know; the Leader is Gwen and the jewels on the necklace are the stolen stones. Scarlett never took that thing off. Damn—she knows! Gwen knows about all of this," he said, rubbing his temples.

"Hey . . . are you okay?" I asked. "You keep touching your head. Are you feeling alright?"

"Yeah, I'm okay. It's just a slight headache. I keep having these thoughts, weird ideas. I feel like someone's tapping into my brain or something."

I looked down at the stone in my hand. "Earlier today, when Habock and I first arrived, I had heart pains. I thought maybe it was because Black Scarlett had almost discovered me. But then later on, I saw myself in my bedroom mirror and I had no reflection. Sparks, I think it's these stones. I think they're making us sick."

"It must have some control over whoever's around it," he said.

"And the burden of pain," I added. "Yet, I'm feeling great now. Maybe the stone doesn't work on me anymore. I feel as if that light helped remove all my doubts. I don't think Gwen is behind my new confidence, I think someone else is." In my mind, I knew what to do. "I should hold on to this."

We both stared at the jewel in my palm. But then something happened; my hand began to shake. "Sparks—"

A dim light appeared around the edges of the stone as the black polished surface began to illuminate.

"Maybe you should put that thing down," he said, with a worried look.

"Wait, how would you describe the shape of this stone?"

His answer was quick. "It looks like a broken arrowhead."

"My thoughts, exactly. Doesn't it look like its pointing somewhere?"

He agreed.

Peeking out from behind the bushes, I saw that we were alone. "Come on—get your stuff. We need to find the others. I think I might know what's going on."

He shook his head. "I don't know about this, Scar."

"Trust me, Sparks—I have an idea!"

KEEP IN TIME

BLACK SCARLETT STOPPED as her feet reached the edge of the tunnel. "This is it, Habock, this is the entrance."

He looked around, searching for any signs of followers. "I think we're alone."

"We're right beneath Grinstone Gail," she said, peering into the underground walkway.

"You and Sparks dug this?"

"Yeah, it took us a while but it leads right to the edge of Velvet Elm. We figured that if the forests were taken, there'd be no way for us to make it through them. So, we created an alternative route."

"Scarlett—this is very good. Smart thinking."

"Thanks. It's small and narrow but it'll work. At least I'm hoping it does. So—what's the plan?"

With cautious steps, he walked into the tunnel. Slowly, he turned to face her. "We stay quiet, we walk fast and we don't look back."

"Okay . . . but wait," she hesitated. "Can you tell me one thing? Why did you make me leave my necklace back there?"

Habock sighed. "Sentiments aside, that necklace was not a gift. The one who gave it to you intended it for something else altogether."

"What do you mean by that?"

"Nevermind," he said. "Look Scarlett, when we get to the end of thi tunnel, you're going to learn everything that you need to know. It's tim you understood that."

She yielded to his knowledge. "Then tell me, what is at the other end of this tunnel that I don't already know?"

"Nothing but danger. You've been strong up until now, Scarlett, and need you to hold on to that strength. I can't do this alone. I'm not trying to blindly lead you but if I tell you what else is waiting out there, you migh not go."

She didn't answer.

"Scarlett—are you listening to me?" he said, tapping her foot with hi paw.

With a simple nod, she responded. "I'm listening."

"It's pretty dark in there—so I'll lead the way."

"Okay."

Habock walked ahead as Black Scarlett followed closely behind. Her hands pressed against the earth as she moved quietly step by step. Although Habock's courage was leading the way, Black Scarlett's determination was following in spades.

As they sifted through the mild December air, neither one of them spoke. Their journey thus far, was silent, without words. Arriving at their destination undetected, was all either of them wanted.

As they curved around one of the bends in the tunnel, Habock heard something above them. "Stop," he whispered. He looked back and saw several stones falling from the ceiling. His attention focused on the roof of dirt above them.

"What is it?"

Habock didn't answer. His eyes remained glued to the ceiling.

Black Scarlett looked up and watched with him. She then peered over at Habock and saw that his eyes were now closed; his attention was drawn to something else.

"Someone or something is close, I can feel it," he said.

Just then, the ground began to tremble above them. "That doesn't sound good," she murmured. "What do you think is going on up there?"

Habock's concern was obvious. "I don't know . . . but I don't like it."

The two remained noiseless as they listened. Activity in the ceiling was momentarily suspended as the stream of falling stones ceased.

"Okay—let's go," he said.

A few minutes passed without any interruptions. Habock's senses were on high alert, though. He could detect the slightest vibration in the ground, or change in scenery. It was comparable to having a trigger-happy motion sensor around. The best place for Black Scarlett to be—was close to him.

"Habock, I think . . . ." She got part way through the sentence when Habock turned and stopped her.

"Shhh . . ." he said. "Do you hear that?"

She nodded. A wispy, buzzing sound moved through the tunnel towards them. Together they watched as the darkened space filled with neon colour.

"Robberflies!" Just as Habock spoke the words, the ceiling above them began to quake. "They know we're here—they'll rip the tunnel right open if they have to!"

The ground now shook vigorously above them as they looked on in fear. Then in a sudden burst, a horde of Robberflies flew onto the scene, instantly swarming them.

Black Scarlett took off her backpack and swung it in all directions. "I can't see!"

Habock was unresponsive.

"Where are you?" she screamed. Peering through the cloud of colour, she saw Habock swatting the mass of insects with his tail and body. Instantly, she thrashed her bag from side to side to reach him. "Get out of here! Get away from us!" she yelled.

Then as quickly as they came, they disappeared, leaving a trail of pink, blue and green behind them. As they left, the shaking stopped.

Black Scarlett looked down at her frightened friend and saw his body heaving, heavily. "Are you okay?"

Habock said nothing. He just stared at the back of the tunnel as he tried to catch his breath.

"What is it?" she said.

"Oh no!"

She turned to look. "Habock . . . what is that?"

Behind them, coming from the entrance of the tunnel, was a ribbon of red. The space around them began to warm as a veil of water now rushed towards them.

Her eyes widened and her skin shivered in response to the fire that approached. "Oh . . . my . . . God!"

Habock turned to face her. "We've got to get out of here—NOW!"

Black Scarlett's face was pale and her legs shook with fear. She knew very well how long the tunnel was and how they hadn't even ventured half-way through it. Her mind kicked into high gear though, when the first wave of water swam past her shoes. Quickly, she lifted her feet. She looked at Habock and their eyes locked.

"You can do this!" he said, reassuring her. He then vaulted onto her shoulders and dug his claws into her coat.

"Scarlett—RUN!"

LIGHT, BRIGHT AND READY TO FIND

EELING THE WEIGHT of the spy's eyes all around us, Sparks and I walked quietly down the road. We were following the tiny beacon that sat in the palm of my hand as it led us into the fog.

"Here we go," I whispered.

A deep haze covered us as we disappeared into the cloud.

"Sparks—where are you?"

A stream of red light appeared, moving like a laser in all directions. "I'm right behind you—I turned the flashlight on."

"Okay, stay close."

"The closer the better," he said.

Although I couldn't see his face, I could tell that he was smiling.

"So tell me something, Sparks. What's your real name?"

He hesitated. "It's . . . Ainsley." His voice was low and I sensed that he was embarrassed.

"Ainsley—that's a nice name. Why don't you use that?"

"I don't know, I guess I prefer Sparks—it's tougher."

"Well, where did the name 'Sparks' come from?" I asked.

"My friends gave me that name because I used to light firecrackers in my backyard and not just on holidays if you catch my drift. I don't do it as much as I used to, but I still carry them around with me in case the spirit moves me. I just love that explosive sound they make when they blast . . . you know . . . the fire within your ears. It's kind of a fetish."

"Firecrackers, huh? Your neighbours must love you. So, your name is Ainsley. I like Ainsley—it's nicer."

"That doesn't sound like something you'd say, Scar."

"Well, I guess you've got a lot to learn about me, then," I smiled.

"When we get out of this mess, I will."

Looking down, I could see the small black stone brimming with light as it pointed to somewhere up ahead. "I think we're close, the light is getting brighter."

"Closer to what?"

"To its Mothership," I laughed.

As we walked, I learned more about Sparks. I discovered that he was actually a good student; half of his classes were advanced. His lack of respect for authority however landed him in detention quite often. At home, he rebelled against the clock, much like me. We had similar personalities. I guess that's why I was drawn to him at school, regardless of Habock's meddling.

Sparks and I were two sides of the same coin. But I had strayed into a darker place than he did. Thankfully, he was there to pull me out.

I stopped suddenly when the stone began moving in my hand, much like one of those Mexican jumping beans I used to play with as a kid. "Sparks—something's happening. It's moving . . . the stone is moving."

I took one step forward and instantly felt something beneath my foot. Kneeling down, I felt the ground with my other hand. I couldn't make out what was under my shoe until I touched it. "I found it!"

"Found what?" he said, bending down beside me. He pointed the light at the ground.

"It's Scarlett's necklace," I said, picking it up. Then, with a magnetic-like force, the jewel leapt out of my hand and attached itself to the strand of stones. "Whoa—did you see that?"

Sparks just stared at the necklace. "It's like it wanted to be found."

As I stood to survey our surroundings, I noticed that the fog was becoming lighter. "Help me put this on."

"What? I don't think that's a good idea," he said. "Look what it did to your future self. It's dangerous, it'll control you."

"I don't think so, Sparks. Gwen may have deceived us before but she forgot one thing: human compassion. She's like this robot for all we know, with all her drones to help her. But you were able to find and help Black Scarlett, and right now, I think someone is trying to help *me*."

I began to walk ahead on the road. The fog broke ahead of me and I called for Sparks to follow.

As he entered the clearing, he shook his head. "It's just that I lost you once and I don't want that to happen again."

"It won't, because not only are we going to right what's wrong, but we're going to save everyone by doing it."

"That's your pride talking," he smiled.

"No—this time it's my intuition."

CAUGHT OR FOUND?

PARKS AND I arrived at the edge of Grinstone Gail. As we approached the woods, we could feel the force of the wind drawing us in. My hand in his, we descended down into a ditch just offside the forest. We climbed down the slope as Sparks led me towards the opening of his hidden tunnel.

"This is the entrance. Wait . . ." he stopped. "Something feels off . . ." He turned to face the clearing and then looked around.

"What's wrong?" I asked.

"I don't know but something feels weird."

He looked inside the opening and saw traces of water on the ground. He stepped inside and felt the walls.

I followed him and placed my hands on the sides of the tunnel. "It's warm in here . . . and wet. There's hardly any water on the ground though, just some puddles. It's almost like it was flooded."

"Oh no, that's not good," he said.

"What is it—what's wrong?"

"It means that someone powerful was here that shouldn't have been. It makes sense though, since Scar was wearing the necklace when we dug this out."

"Gwen was here?" I needed a moment to organize my thoughts.

Sparks was obviously frazzled by this new revelation. Again, he rubbed his forehead.

I watched his actions closely. It seemed that the more convinced I was that our mission would succeed, Sparks grew more disheartened. I told myself earlier though, that I wouldn't allow my emotions to sidetrack me. I had to continue on. Fairy tale or not, I was going to persevere.

I believed that I was meant to find the necklace, just as I believed that Habock was the one who had left it for me. Somehow, he must have known that I was following him.

Now we had discovered that my sister Gwen—the Leader—had found the tunnel and had most likely flushed Habock and Black Scarlett out. Hopefully, they were safe but right now I wasn't too sure. If Gwen had caused the accident that took my father's life, then there was no telling what she would do with other innocents.

I however, wasn't going to let this new kink in our plans upset me. I was done being sisterly.

Looking at Sparks, I knew what I had to do. "You and I are going to go ahead with our plan. Whoever's responsible for giving me this gift of fearlessness, probably did it so that I could help the others. If my instincts are right, then the necklace won't give away my location or what we talked about. So, it's time we threw the bad guys a red herring. Are you with me?"

He complied.

"You go and wait at the edge of Finlake Fir. I'm going to make my way to Velvet Elm and find the others. I'll help them however I can. Once I'm finished there, I'll meet you at Finlake and help you destroy the mirrors."

"Okay." He then placed the flashlight in my hand. "But there's one thing you should know. If you find your future self, be wary."

I wasn't expecting him to say that. "Why?" I asked.

"If Gwen has the chance to destroy one of you, then it will be you, not the future you."

I wasn't too sure what he was getting at or why he was telling me this now. "Why would that make a difference?"

"Because, Scar, if she decides that she doesn't need you around anymore, she'll wipe both of you out if she destroys the past. If she kills you, then the future you will cease to exist. If there are two of you to contend with—then it'll be you that she goes after."

I just stared at him. I hadn't thought of that. Here I was, worried about everyone else, when I hadn't even thought about my own future

line. I nodded my head in a knowing gesture. And to show Sparks tha
I wasn't disturbed by this new information, I simply said, "Okay—I'l
remember that."

He took my hands. "Please be careful." His eyes were tender as h
spoke, but I could tell that he was still troubled.

I had to remain strong in my beliefs. "You need to get away from thi
necklace—that's why I'm going to take it with me. It can't hurt me and
won't let it hurt anyone else."

He smiled at me. "You're incredibly stubborn you know."

"Yeah, yeah, tell me something I don't know." I then wrapped my arm
around his body and squeezed. "I'll be fine, I promise."

With that, I turned and walked into the tunnel.

A MAZE, AMAZING, IN AMAZEMENT

Y WALK THROUGH the tunnel was tranquil and so far, without delay. I remained soundless as I held the flashlight in front of me. I wondered what had happened inside these walls before I arrived. They were dripping with warm water. The noise echoed through my ears as each drop met the ground.

My feet skirted around the puddles as I made my way to the other end of the tunnel. Thank heavens I had a flashlight, the area was incredibly dark.

As I went around one of the bends, I saw something in front of the red beam. A small, still figure lay on the ground ahead of me. Slowly, I approached, not knowing whether it was meant to be found or not. The closer I got, the more I understood what it was. It was one of those flying insects I saw earlier on the road. "A Robberfly—a spy!" I said, kneeling beside it.

There was no life in this little animal. It just lay there, motionless.

Looking it over, I realized that its wings had been singed. "Poor little guy." A moment of sadness passed through me when I thought about its demise—it had been burned by its own maker. That seemed strange to me but perhaps it was an accident.

Then I thought about what might have happened. The water in the tunnel was warm which made me think about Finlake and Blazenridge forests. Their elements were being harnessed.

Just then, its little body began to emit a soft pink hue as its legs and wings came to life. Gently, it fluttered on the ground as it looked all around. It peered up at me.

I stretched my hand out to touch the insect and it stepped onto my palm. Timidly, it walked along the tips of my fingers. It then lifted itself in front of my face and stared at me. I didn't move. I only watched. Its miniature wings flapped up and down as it floated on the air. Then, in a sudden thrust, it elevated itself high above my head and flew out the back of the tunnel, leaving a pink sparkly trail behind it.

For whatever reason, I wasn't worried about the tiny spy. I felt as if this Robberfly would protect my secrecy.

Regardless of our encounter, I continued on.

*   *   *

Forty minutes had flown by and I was still in the tunnel, with no idea whether I was nearing the end of it or not.

Oddly enough, the tunnel I was in reminded me of the pumpkin farm in our town. Every Halloween, I would venture off with my friends to visit the pumpkin patch and enjoy the festivities offered to us. And every year I would get lost in the corn maze—every single year. I was without a doubt, the most hopeless person there. Even small children could find their way out without the accompaniment of a parent. Not me, though. I always got lost.

I just laughed it off. Perhaps children used their innocence as an escape tool, whereas I always calculated my exit, strategically. My way never worked of course, and my friends always had to come in to rescue me.

I giggled at the thought of it, for here I was inside a one-way maze, looking for a way out. "Who gets lost in a tunnel? There's only one way in and one way out. Only this could happen to me."

On a positive note, I wasn't claustrophobic. That was a good thing too, because the tunnel was very narrow. It was only five feet wide and six feet high. I guess Sparks and Black Scarlett didn't care about space; they were most likely concerned with the practicality and usefulness of its construction. The tunnel was a means to an end.

As I rounded another bend, I saw a light ahead of me. "What is that?" Then I grasped what it was—it was the end of the tunnel.

Senses alert, I looked around. There were no stragglers or followers. Not even that flying bug came back—there was no sign of it.

A large smile chased the frown from my face when I realized how close I was to the rim of the forest. "Velvet Elm!"

With discreet movements, I made my way to the tunnel's opening. Each move I made had to be smart and deliberate. There was no room for error in this maze. I didn't know what awaited me out there, I had to be cautious.

As I trudged forward, the beauty of the night came into view. Hidden, I remained inside the tunnel as I gazed out at the stars above me. I was mesmerized by the twinkling in the sky. But now, I could feel the energy of the moon. Avari's light seeped through the trees ahead of me. Her light touched the ground as the area outside the tunnel sparkled in her glow. The eclipse was now over.

I was slightly apprehensive to leave the safety of my enclosure but when I saw the trail of water leading into the woods, I knew what I had to do.

Slowly, I stepped out into the clearing and looked around. I was alone. I turned off the flashlight and made my way up to the forest's edge. Turning back, I saw the trees bending inside Grinstone Gail. The gale-force winds were causing them to lean dramatically in angles that were unnatural. There was no way I would have made it safely through that forest. It looked like a hurricane back there.

The tunnel had supported my cause. It had provided a safe pathway beneath the forest. I could feel a slight breeze in the air as my hair lifted off my shoulders. The winds thankfully, had been left behind. It was now time to move on.

I stiffened my spine. "You can do this, Scarlett. You can."

My first few steps were guarded but as I entered the woods, I knew that my feet were on solid ground. I felt a positive energy flow through me as if the forest sensed the good in my heart. It welcomed me with open branches.

Each additional step was placed with confidence, and for the next ten minutes I walked with courage and conviction. I felt a strong connection to the earth I was treading on. I now had no fear of proceeding.

As I brushed past the leaves and branches, I heard a voice directly ahead of me. Make that, three voices. With all the muffling I could conjure, I crept forward toward the sounds.

The voices came into view as I stood behind a large tree, peeking out. The trees opened into a clearing and for the first time since leaving the house, I saw Gwen. I heard the unmistakable sound of her voice. She was pacing back and forth in a royal manner. She exuded power.

I was somewhat stunned by the clothing she now adorned. The adolescent costume I was accustomed to seeing her in was gone. Instead she wore a long flowing black robe that covered her body. It trailed behind her like a darker version of a wedding gown. Her face was hidden by the ebony hood that shrouded her head. For the first time ever, I got chills just looking at her.

Her voice was abrasive and filled with irritation. It appeared that she was talking to someone or something.

I had to get closer to see.

With muted movement, I grazed past the leaves, trying not to trip over the large roots beneath them. I then bent down on the forest floor and peered through the foliage. Attentively, I listened to see what I could learn.

One of the other voices spoke. I looked through the green and saw that it was Habock. To the left of him was Black Scarlett. They had been found.

Although they had been captured, they didn't seem to be in any immediate danger. Nothing on their bodies was tied. Evidently, they were able to move freely. But instead they remained still, watching Gwen. It seemed odd that they were motionless but when I looked more closely, I saw that they were stuck in something, immobilized. There was an odd material near their feet. Then I realized what it was. Below each of them was a pile of sand.

Gwen spoke again, her words commanding. The more I watched her, the more I understood how this wasn't my sister.

She then paced in my direction and I finally saw what was hidden beneath the hood. Gwen's face was masked behind a layer of silver skin, with a large scar angled above her left eye. I cringed just looking at it—it was the scar from Gwen's soccer injury, or at least that's what I had thought. Her eyes were crimson and filled with pain, giving her an entirely morose appearance.

She hadn't detected me yet but by the looks of things, Habock and Black Scarlett appeared to be part of a trap. Perhaps Gwen knew I was coming or maybe she was just prodding the two of them for answers and secrets. I had to listen to know for sure.

With my ear to the clearing, I concentrated on the voices.

"Where is it? Where is the Star?" Gwen said.

Neither Habock nor Black Scarlett responded. Together they remained tightly lipped, unwilling to talk.

"Speak! Where is the Star?"

Then Black Scarlett spoke. "You'll never find it—it's in a place where darkness can't reach!"

Gwen seemed impermeable to her snide remark. She approached Black Scarlett and smiled. "That was not a clever thing for you to say. I am a sleuth, a detective of secrets. I won't hesitate to hurt you in order to get them."

She backed away and began pacing again. "You know what I'm looking for and what I'm capable of doing to get it. I will spare your lives if you tell me where the Star is hidden."

Behind the leaves, I sat wondering about this 'Star' she was looking for.

Again, the two captives held their tongues.

Gwen was calm as she waited. She must have realized that neither one was going to divulge the location of the object she desired. And so she resulted to time.

"You have exactly seven minutes to tell me, then I will activate the quicksand beneath your feet. Maybe that will inspire you to help." She flashed a wicked grin and then drifted away, into the woods behind them.

I knew at that moment, I had to act. This was the time to be strong. The conversation wasn't about me, so my arrival wasn't expected. Or at least that's what I hoped. I looked around the clearing and saw no one else around.

I darted out from behind the trees towards where Habock and Black Scarlett were standing. Apparently, I surprised them both.

Habock was ecstatic. "Scarlett—you came!"

"Oh my God—who are you?" Black Scarlett cried. Her eyes practically bulged out of her head.

"It's okay, Scarlett. She's here to help!" Habock said, reassuring her. "You *are* here to help, right?"

"Yes—I'm here to help. Okay, I can't explain in full right now but I'm you from the past," I said, looking into her eyes. "About two-and-a-half years in the past, actually."

I glanced over at Habock and saw that he was smiling. "It's good to see you. I see you got the necklace."

"Yes, thank you for that. How did you know I would find it?"

"It was all part of the plan," he said, with a grin.

Again I thought, *what a good little actor he was.* "Look, Scarlett—we don't have much time. Gwen is the Leader, as you already know, and she's going to come back in a couple of minutes. I need you to trust me," I said.

She looked over at Habock and he concurred. "Do what she says."

"Tell me—what's this 'Star' that she's looking for and where can I find it?"

Her answer was forthwith. "It's called the Star of Hope. Avari told us that the Star needs to be placed in the Tree of Life inside the golden web at the top. The tree is in the centre of Velvet Elm—it's the oldest one in the forest. Once the Star is in the web, the forests will be reclaimed by Good. It will stop Gwen."

"And that means we'll be able to recapture the elements," I added.

"Yes."

"Alright—so where is the Star?"

"I don't know yet," she said.

"The Star of Hope lies within both of you," Habock answered. "It's inside your hearts. Gwen can't touch it in there."

I smiled at both of them. "Okay—I know what to do." I stretched out my hand and placed it over Habock's back. A ray of light illuminated his body, freeing him from the sand. "Now you can move."

Paw by paw, he lifted his toes. "Thank you."

"You're welcome. But I need you to stay still."

"How did you do that?" my future self asked.

"I don't know—it just came to me," I said, stepping in front of her. I then placed my right hand over her heart. "Your turn."

Her body began to glitter as the power inside me passed into her. "You should be able to move now."

Carefully, she stepped off of the sand as she regained control of her body. She shook her head in bewilderment. "I don't understand."

"Trust me—it's okay. Now, we can't all run because we won't have much of a head start. So, we're gonna have to do something else."

"What do you need?" she said.

I glanced around the clearing and then looked back at my mirror image. "I have a plan," I said, with confidence. "Give me all your clothes."

SIGHT UNSEEN

WEN CREPT BACK into the clearing as she reappeared in front of her captives. "I heard voices," she started. "I know that at least one of you has the answer I seek."

Her steel-grey skin shimmered in the night, like a star out of whack. It was difficult to look at her and yet, her darkness was somewhat compelling.

I watched as she now stood in front of Habock playing with her fingers. "The girl doesn't know, does she? But I bet her guide does. Apparently, I was speaking to the wrong person."

Immediately, the hairs on the back of my neck lifted. *Person? What did she mean by that?* My gaze wandered to the side, as my face remained still in place. I listened intently to each and every word.

"That's right, kitty. I know all about you. You're a long way from home. It's quite interesting actually—they say that cats have nine lives. I wonder if there's any truth to that." She backed away from him. "Part of it must be true—you've died before," she cackled.

My eyelids expanded as this information entered my brain. I felt an immediate cognitive overflow as each interaction I'd had with Habock, overtook my senses. The situation was becoming clear to me: his eyes, his knowledge, his kindness and especially his purpose for being here. *Oh my God!*

Gwen spoke with zeal. "So let's see how many lives you have left." With a twirl of her finger, the sand beneath Habock's paws began to move.

"Wait!" I said. "I have what you want—don't hurt him."

Gwen turned to me with a strange expression on her face. "Do I sense a bit of empathy?"

"I just don't want anyone else to get hurt. I have the answer you want—leave him alone," I said.

She hesitated. "Very well." With the wave of her hand, the stirring of sand came to a halt. She then walked in front of me. "So, we have a hero. For your sake my dear, I hope you do have the answer."

"The Star . . ." I paused. "The Star that you're looking for is in—"

Habock stopped me. "Scarlett, don't do this!"

Gwen laughed at both of us. "That's cute—you two working together to escape a precarious situation." Her smile then disappeared. "You have one minute to tell me the location of the Star or else you're both going to a sandy grave."

"The Star . . . is somewhere in the forest." My tone then turned a sharp curve. "And you, my dear, will never get your creepy hands on it." My words were assertive and towering. Power controlled my body.

Blood red eyes stared back at me, as suspicion now permeated through Gwen's evil skin. "Is that so?"

"Yes," I said. "And in a few minutes, you will no longer have dominion over these forests. Your time here is done." I was ready for anything. Body language was very telling and although this monster had occupied Gwen's soul, its body was still human. She exhibited features and expressions that I could competently interpret. I was, after all, a teenager.

Right now, Gwen's expression was surprise. *Good,* I thought. *This is exactly what I wanted.*

"You're not her—you're the other one," she barked.

My plan was working. "Wow, you found me out. Sorry to keep you waiting but I had a few other things to tend to in this time. Thanks for being so patient."

Apparently, she was unequipped to deal with my humour.

"Oh, come on now," I joked. "Like you didn't see this coming." I then unzipped my coat to reveal the necklace. "Oh, right—I guess you *didn't* see this coming, did you!"

I looked down at Habock, his eyes were stoic.

"This is the necklace you gave Scarlett—how nice of you. I guess you forgot to mention that it was made of stolen stones. Yeah, I put two and two together. Not only were they Seeing stones, but in the hands of evil, they controlled others such as myself."

Gwen said nothing. Her fiery stare glared at both of us.

Simultaneously, Habock and I descended off the piles of sand. "What you didn't plan for is that in the hands of Good, this necklace could be used against you. Yeah, I figured that one out, too. It's amazing how an uncorrupted mind can work. See—you haven't gotten to me yet. Your powers are pretty much useless—especially against Avari."

"No!" she cried.

"Yep—I had a little help from a friend. You lose!"

I could tell that Gwen's stock was plummeting; she hadn't expected any of this. I, on the other hand, was savouring every minute of our witty banter.

I turned to Habock. "Do you think that was enough time?"

"I think so. She should be there by now," he answered.

Gwen was infuriated by the turn of events. "You fooled me! You won't get away with this!"

I placed my hands on my hips and threw on my best winning smile. "I think we already have."

Seconds later, a black curtain wafted through the trees as it entered into the clearing. Hundreds of Mirrorwalkers appeared as they stood behind their leader, waiting for instruction.

"Uh oh . . . I didn't see this coming," I whispered to Habock.

"We have to get out of here," he said, from the corner of his mouth.

"Perhaps your victory was a bit . . . premature?" Gwen beamed. She looked upon the eyes of her warriors. "I guess we'll have to lessen their odds."

Hordes of black capes stood before us, breathing heavily into the night. One by one, they began to scream a deafening cry.

I raised my hands to cup my ears as the bellowing sounded all around us. But the more they screamed, the stronger I got.

"Habock—get behind me," I said.

"Scarlett—we need to get to the tree!"

As he spoke, Gwen unleashed her band of drones. "GET THEM!" she howled.

"We can't outrun them, Habock!"

As the outpouring of evil approached, I held up my hands and yelled "NO!"

Suddenly, a solid wall of cloud appeared around Habock and I preventing chase from the predator. I peered into the silver lining but could see very little. I heard them though, as they pounded frantically to get through to us.

"That's so cool! They'll never get around that!"

"Come on, Scarlett—we have to go!" Habock said with urgency. "This won't protect us for long."

Promptly, I turned. Habock was already heading into the trees. "Wait for me!" I cried.

Together, we raced through the woods to the Tree of Life, hoping that Black Scarlett had made it there safely.

"Wow—I can't believe that I did that!"

Habock continued running. He said nothing along the way.

The barrier I had created was my attempt at evading capture. I knew that somewhere inside of me, was the power to block the enemy's attack. I did so by tapping into Avari's energy—that was the only answer I could come up with. All I had to do was channel my inner desires.

A powerful tool Avari turned out to be. Just how powerful exactly? I was about to find out.

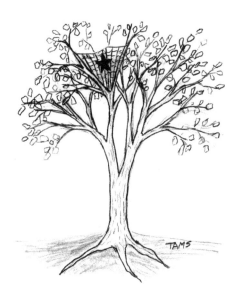

TREE OF LIFE

Y PLAN WAS simple: switch places with Black Scarlett and send her to the Tree of Life. I would remain with Habock, to stall Gwen. This would in turn, give my future self the time she needed to get to the tree.

Now, here we were, running as fast as we could through the woods to get to her.

"We're almost there!" Habock yelled, as his body bounded over the roots and leaves. "I can see it from here!"

Although the adrenalin inside of me was filling my mind with spirit, it was nice to hear the optimism in his voice. I now knew who he was. His feline body could no longer mask the truth. Gwen had given his secret away.

My legs were pumping with ferocity as I sped after him.

Up ahead, was another clearing. As Habock and I burst out into the opening, we were startled to see Black Scarlett standing before us. Behind her stood Gwen, shielded in darkness.

Below Black Scarlett's feet was a mass of swirling sand. Her body began to sink into the ground as the material slowly swallowed her.

"NO!" Habock cried.

She was screaming though a thick black gag and her hands were drawn behind her back.

"Interesting parlour trick back there," Gwen smiled. "Too bad it couldn't save yourself. I guess I don't need her anymore since I have you."

Black Scarlett thrust her body in all directions as she tried desperately to escape the pull beneath her.

Anger surged through my heart as I watched my future self being tortured. Hot fire rumbled inside of me and I lifted my hands towards Gwen. "NOOOO!" I screamed.

A bolt of white lightning shot from my palms as it blasted the enemy's body into the air. I watched as she fell into the trees, somewhere off in the distance.

Habock stood beside me as I looked on, delighted that my attack had been successful.

Black Scarlett shrieked through the gag as she lay on the ground, surrounded by sand. Quickly, Habock and I ran to her side.

"Release!" I said, waving my hand above her.

The sand discharged her body from its grainy clutch as she gently rolled onto her back. Her mouth and arms were freed from constraint. Peering up at me, she wiggled her jaws and fingers. "Thank you," she said, coughing.

"Scarlett—look at me," Habock said, calmly.

I glanced over at him. "What?"

"Your eyes, Scarlett—what's happening to you?"

"Nothing's happening to me. What's wrong with my eyes?"

"They're white!" he said, surprised.

"So what?" I laughed.

"Scarlett—I think some power is taking over you."

"Don't be silly, Habock. I just fired the enemy into the sky to save my future self—isn't that a good thing?"

He didn't seem convinced by my answer.

"I'm fine, I'm resilient."

"That's what worries me," he said.

"Habock, we have more important things to worry about." I stretched out my hand to help Black Scarlett off of the ground. "Are you okay?"

"I think so," she said.

I knew that we only had a small window of time, so I cut the pleasantries short. "Is this the tree?"

"Yes," Habock said, walking towards it. "One of you must climb it."

I sent my gaze upward to assess the old Elm. It was narrow, spindly but thick, and charcoal black. It looked like it had already been through several wars. I figured it was roughly thirty feet high—easy enough to climb. *What stories this tree could tell*, I thought.

"I think you should go," Black Scarlett said. "If anything happens to you down here, then our line will be wiped out."

I understood immediately. "I agree."

"I'll stay here in case something happens," Habock said. "Be fast, I don't know how long we can hold Gwen off for if she comes back."

"Okay," I said.

Habock gave me a tender look. "Be careful."

Then, in an unexpected turn of events, a wave of heat entered the tree. Its colour came alive with red flames as unbridled fire swept through the trunk and up into the branches.

"She's here!" Habock yelled.

"Sooner than you expected," Gwen's voice appeared behind us.

We all turned in surprise.

Habock looked up at the sky. "Scarlett—get to the web! The alignment is starting!"

My eyes turned from Gwen as they caught the first leg of the spider crossing Avari. "Oh no!" Clear as day, we could see the animal creeping over the moon's surface. And in our line of sight, was Arachne's constellation.

"GO!" Habock hollered. He hissed at Gwen and then leapt into the air, landing on her chest. He clawed incessantly at her face as she wailed aloud.

Black Scarlett ran towards Gwen, knocking her over. She landed on top of her, pinning her to the ground. Like two wild animals, they ravaged their prey.

I knew what I had to do. I looked at the burning tree before me and raised my hands. "Water!" I commanded.

A small cloud formed over the tree as tiny droplets of water began to fall. One by one, the flames were quelled as a hush fell over the branches.

Looking behind me, I saw that Gwen was still under attack. I hurried over to the tree, felt the limbs with my fingers and began climbing. The water had immediately squelched the fire and returned the tree's temperature to normal. The power inside of me had worked instantly. In the time it took to snap my fingers, the tree had returned to its natural form. Just a faint sizzle could be heard as small streams of smoke exited the bark.

With each step, I felt stronger. Although trouble lay behind me, I knew in the back of my mind, that success would come to us. I only hoped that it didn't come at a cost.

Carefully, I ascended through the branches. Although the tree had been ablaze for only a minute, the smell of charred wood was strong.

As I neared the top of the tree, I looked down at the ground. Gwen, Habock and Black Scarlett were no longer visible. Where were they? It upset me not to see them there. But then my eyes were drawn to an object above me. It glimmered beneath the stars and I knew at once—it was the web. I lifted myself onto the branch beside it and gazed at its small construction. The web was golden-brown with shiny fibres interlaced within each other. It was roughly two feet around and sat nestled in between two branches. It was beautiful.

As I reached out to touch it, I felt a strange patter in my heart.

"Oh great—not this again!" When I placed my hand over my chest, it began to glow. Removing my palm, I realized that my fingers were now holding a round light. "Oh my God—it's the Star!"

A voice beneath me shrieked, "NO!"

When I looked down, I saw Gwen screaming. Out of her hand, shot a ball of red hot fire. It raged towards me through the air. Quickly, I ducked to avoid its path as the Star slipped through my fingers.

In sheer panic, I reached into the air and grabbed it with both hands, nearly losing my balance along the way. I leaned back and secured my footing. *That was close. Too close.*

Three more fireballs flew towards me as Gwen unleashed her power. I dodged each one, just barely. I had nowhere to go.

She was determined to stop me but I knew I had to complete my task. I was losing my cool and was now at the end of my tether.

"ENOUGH!" my voice thundered down as a thick protective screen encircled the tree.

Gwen continued to cast fireballs towards me but was thwarted every time. She looked on with extreme vexation.

The Star was now guiding my hands towards the web. With both palms curled around it, I placed the glowing sphere into the woven fibres, where it latched on securely. In doing so, the tree began to move.

As I tried to sturdy myself, the branch began to sway back and forth. "Uh oh."

I gripped onto the nearest branch as waves began to pulsate through the ground. Large ripples followed along the surface as the waves scattered in all directions.

Faster and faster, the branch moved with every motion. At one point, I thought it would disengage from the tree.

Looking down, I saw the ground moving frantically as Nature crumbled along the forest floor. I thought I was in the midst of an earthquake. Then like a rocket shooting through my ears, the air around me filled with lightning clatter. A sheet of light broke through the night sky as the tree trembled from side to side.

I wrapped my limbs around the branch, holding it snugly. There was no way I was letting go. Like a Boa Constrictor, my embrace was tight.

A moment later, the tree's movement began to cease. I unlocked my bones and looked around. Everything had stopped moving. Almost everything, that is.

Below me, I heard the voice of the enemy, seething. "You may have released the forests from my grip but you will not release theirs."

Now, lying beside the tree, were Habock and Scarlett. Their bodies were still, as if they were sleeping. Hovering over them, was my nemesis.

"What did you do to them!" I roared.

"No, no—it's what *you* did," she berated me with her finger. "You left them all alone with me. Oh, and your friend Sparks sends his regrets. He's with me now. I'm sure he'll be sorry that he missed this, though."

Her existence was entirely caustic. I felt sick just listening to her. With each word, she taunted and belittled me. My guarded shell began to crack as my body began to weaken.

The anger I had demonstrated earlier was replaced with grief and regret. Gwen was right, this *was* my fault. I should have stayed with Sparks—I knew something was wrong when I left him. And now the other two were within in her talons.

"If you hurt them—I swear to God I will destroy you!"

She smiled up at me. "You know where to find us. Try not to take too long. I'm not responsible for what might happen—you are!"

With that, she swung her long robe over the bodies and disappeared into the night air.

Oh God! Tears streamed along my face as I began to climb down the tree. What had I done? I was responsible for this mess, if only I had been stronger. *I should have let Black Scarlett climb the tree. I could have protected her more that way. And poor Habock—he trusted me to do th right thing.*

My body slumped in despair as I descended over the branches. I felt my heart giving out. The confidence that drove me here was disappearing.

As my feet touched the ground, I collapsed onto my knees. I sat there holding my head in my hands for what seemed like eternity, wondering what to do next.

Then I heard a gentle voice from above. And I knew that I wasn' alone.

HELP IN OTHER WAYS

HE VOICE I now heard had a cottony feel to it; my thoughts of turmoil were comforted by its tranquil tone. As I lifted my head to look, the tears that I harboured escaped down my cheeks. They were, no doubt, in search of a new home.

I opened my eyes to the softness and saw the brilliant glow of the Earth's moon. Its emerald green eyes shone down with tenderness. It was talking to me.

"You have come so far, Scarlett. You must not give up. You saved me from a dreadful fate and I am indebted to you."

"Are you . . . Avari?" I said, timidly.

"Yes." Her voice was sweet, honey-like.

"You're the talking moon. I'm sorry—it's just that I didn't believe you existed. Not like this anyway."

"I understand," she said. "You have experienced a great deal of change."

Again, my face became wet with the dribble of tears. "I've lost my friends. Gwen has them and I don't know what she's going to do with them. And I don't feel as confident as I did before." My speech began to slur. "I don't know what to do."

Avari smiled down. "You don't know the strength that lies inside o you."

"I don't know what's inside me anymore," I sobbed.

"Listen to me, Scarlett. You put on the necklace and it helped you—a did I. My strength and power helped you get this far."

"I assumed that was you."

"Yes. You had a taste of my powers, Scarlett—pure white light. Now you can do this with your own power—from within. You have proven yourself, my dear."

I sniffled. "How do you know that?"

"Because I know someone who cares about you deeply, and he would not have brought you here if he did not believe in you."

"It's Habock," I said. "He's my father—isn't he?"

"Yes."

"How is that even possible? They co-existed in my house. How could they be in two different bodies?"

"It's magic," Avari glistened.

I didn't know what to say.

"Habock is counting on you. We all are. My path of light shows, that *you* are the one who will defeat the Leader and change all of this. We need you. Believe in your heart—let it prove to you how strong it is."

Slowly, I stood. "Do you really think I'm capable of this? Habock thought that something was wrong with me—he said that my eyes had changed. And I felt different, too. I knew it. Something was growing inside of me—I acted with rage. It was the only way to defeat the enemy. I would never have hurt anyone who was good."

"I know that." Avari's words were supportive. "You, my dear, can do this without any additional help. Now, take off the necklace."

I looked at her with surprise as I clutched the jewels between my fingers. "But . . ."

"Take it off and see what happens," she insisted.

Behind my neck, my fingers fumbled for the knot Sparks had tied. I released the necklace and held the jewels in my hands. I didn't want to let go.

"It's okay, Scarlett. Let it go."

I flipped my palms over and the stones fell to the ground. Oddly, a great weight lifted from my body.

"The necklace helped you in your search, but now there is no need for it," Avari said. "True power, comes from within."

I sighed and looked away as the tears I had shed completed their journey to the ground. "I guess we'll have to see."

With enforced kindness, she continued. "The last part of your voyage will take you to Finlake Forest, where you will call for the mirrors. They will be hidden from view so you must bring them to sight. After the mirrors appear, destroy only two of them. Doing that, will destroy the Mirrorwalkers. Then, you must go back in time to return our world to its rightful path."

"But that's not good enough. I have to destroy the Leader, too," I said.

Avari's capacity for good remained uncompromised even with my urge to kill the Leader. "If you destroy the mirrors then you will take away the Leader's power."

"But she killed my father! How am I supposed to let that go?"

"Scarlett, you are not here to punish evil. You are only here to protect the innocent—remember that." Her tone was genuinely sincere. "When you arrive home, you must destroy Habock's mirror. The Leader will no longer be present in your time."

I wasn't too sure if this made any sense right now but I had no other choice than to believe it.

"Will I ever see you again?"

Avari smiled. "Yes, that is one thing you can be sure of. To prove it, I will grant you one wish. I owe you that much for saving my life."

"A wish?"

"Anything your heart desires, Scarlett."

I thought for a moment. "There's only one thing I want but I'm afraid to say it."

"There is no need to speak it—your heart just told me. Your wish will be granted, Scarlett. Now, the time has come for you to be strong. You must go to the cave."

I took the sleeve of my coat and wiped away any remaining doubts from my face. "How do I get there?"

"Close your eyes," she said, softly.

Avari's voice was familiar to me somehow but my mind was distracted by duty. I focused on her instructions.

"I want you to think of a silver vein, trickling like a brook in front of you."

My mind started to wander past the trees of the forest, alongside a ridge of shallow water. I saw myself in the distance throwing stones into the brook and beneath it was a ribbon of silver. "I see it."

"Follow that silver vein, Scarlett. Let your mind take you to where you are going. Allow your thoughts to move you."

As I thought about the stones in my hands, I began to feel lifted, like a feather drawn upward by the wind. My body meandered along the brook as I carried the stones past the silver vein. Drift by drift, I floated above the water as my mind brought me to another place.

Then, all of a sudden, my senses exploded as the stones burst inside my hands. Awakened by the sound, I opened my eyes to find that I had entered the dragon's lair.

I had arrived at Finlake Forest and was now standing in front of a gravestone, surrounded by sand. Looking around, I understood that I had reached the Leader's secret place of hiding.

Nothing else was here, though. No trees, no Silver Flint—whatever that was. Just this headstone.

As I knelt down to look at the grave, I felt something touch my foot. I brushed it away with my hand but it returned to annoy me. As I turned my head to look, I screamed.

Attached at the base of my ankle, was a hand—without the skin. Pale white bones latched around my foot as they pulled me into the sandy ground.

"Get off of me! GET OFF!" I swatted at it. But my attempt to remain above the surface was useless. The hand was pulling me deeper into the sand. I was going under. Frantically, I reached for something to hold on to but nothing came to my aid.

The last thing I saw was the name of my father on the headstone. *Oh God!* It was then that I finally understood—the Silver Flint was my father's grave.

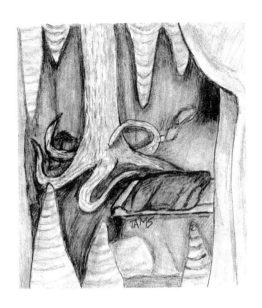

NERVES OF MIGHT, BE STRONG

MY BODY ACHED. I had landed on a hard dirt floor of some sort. I opened my mouth to cough but all that came out was a handful of sand. I rubbed my neck as my eyes soaked up the surroundings. *Where am I?*

Gently, I sat up and patted my ankle. It actually didn't hurt which was a nice surprise. I continued to cough up bits of sand but the amounts were getting smaller. Once I caught my breath, I began to decipher what I was looking at. Light entered from various points in the rocky walls, so thankfully I was able to see. I had landed inside the cave.

I concentrated on the dimensions and made mental notes of the details. The cave was extremely large with lots of space to hide. Unfortunately, there weren't a lot of things to hide behind. I looked at the ceiling which was pretty high up. But when I saw what was hanging down, I shivered. Dangling above my head, were hundreds of large pylons made of rock. And they were all pointed at the cave's floor. *Great—stalactites!* I remembered seeing them with my father when he and I went caving near Algonquin Park. I knew that if one were to land on me, I'd be finished. My hope was that nothing would disturb them.

Scattered along the floor, were their less terrifying brothers—the stalagmites. They didn't bother me as much, but thinking of the cave as a whole—it reminded me of a set of jaws with canine teeth growing all over. Thank goodness the jaws weren't moving.

In the centre of the cave was a tall, ceremonial stand with something draped in black lying on top of it. From my viewpoint, I couldn't tell what it was. Behind me was nothing, but then I spotted Sparks' backpack and I knew that he had to be here somewhere. To my left was open space, lots of it. Ahead of me, was a dirt wall with roots growing all over it. Something was odd though—the roots appeared to be moving. They were creeping, slinking along the wall. When I looked to the right, I saw where the roots were coming from.

Nestled in the wall was an enormous tree. It was the Forest Creeper that I'd heard about in the diary. Tucked deeply within the moving tendrils were Black Scarlett and Sparks. I couldn't tell if they were alive or not. *Oh no!*

I peeled my body off of the ground and made my way towards them. As I approached, one of the roots slithered along the floor behind me and pushed me to the ground. With a heavy thud, I landed. "Ow! What the—"

The long brown arm withdrew itself back to the wall as I lay there watching it. "You've got to be kidding!"

I lifted myself up and slowly this time, walked towards the tree.

In an instant, one of the arms came alive, and with one solid thrust threw me across the floor. This time I landed on my side. As I lay there clutching my ribs, I grimaced. "This is insane!"

Then I heard something across the way. It was coming from within the roots.

Looking over, I saw the eyes of Black Scarlett. She was awake and trying to tell me something. I tried to read her lips but I couldn't quite understand. And then she whispered, "The code!"

I nodded immediately.

In a hushed tone, she informed me that Sparks had a small axe inside his backpack. Responding in code, I told her that I would go and retrieve it.

For a moment, I wondered where the Leader and her drones were. It didn't matter, though—I still had to hurry. I had to rescue Sparks and Black Scarlett as soon as possible if we were going to find the mirrors.

I stood and sprinted to the other side of the cave, and then bent down in front of Sparks' backpack. I sifted through it until I found the axe. It was lying beneath a pile of firecrackers.

My feet hustled over the ground as I ran back to face the arboreal captor. Then I stopped. I figured that it was probably waiting for me to make my next move. I had to be careful. As soundless as possible I crept towards it, with the sharpened blade facing the vines. As I approached, I noticed one of the roots sneaking up behind me. In a flash I turned, forcing the blade downward. The axe cut straight through the root. It shrieked fiercely as it recoiled. The sound it made was hideous, like a small child screaming.

With full force, I rushed towards the wall as I began to chop along Black Scarlett's body. It didn't take long to free her; each arm withdrew as I cut it.

"You got my message," she said, breathing deeply.

"Of course I did, who do you think wrote the code?" I smiled.

"We've got to get Sparks out of there." But as the words left her mouth, five more roots emerged from the wall and knocked us onto the floor.

"Ohhhh . . . this is getting painful," I said, soothing my back with my fingers. A moment later, a hand appeared above my face and helped bring me to my feet. It was Black Scarlett.

"I guess it's my turn to help," she said.

My spine ached. "This is really starting to hurt. Honestly, how are we going to do this?"

"We'll do it together. We need to split its attention. I'll be the diversion—you go get Sparks," she said.

I reached down and picked up the axe. My body was beginning to burn. I now knew that I wouldn't be walking away unscathed. That was the third time I'd been thrown and my soreness was starting to affect my good-hearted pace. Luckily, I hadn't hit my head.

Come on, Scarlett, I told myself. *Hold on just a little bit longer.* I pumped my thoughts with energy, hoping they would pass the information on to my body.

I saw that Black Scarlett was about to go in. She began taunting the roots, jumping in and out of their way as they reached for her. Then without thinking, I ran at the wall and began pounding with the axe to free Sparks. Our plan was working. The only difference was that Sparks wasn't waking up.

As the roots released him, he fell into my arms. The weight of his body nearly toppled me but I managed to keep my footing. "I've got him!" I yelled. I dragged his body across the floor towards his backpack.

Black Scarlett ran over to us. "Sparks! Sparks!" she cried.

I lowered his body onto the ground as far away from the roots as possible. They extended along the ground, but couldn't touch us. There we remained safely out of their reach.

Placing my fingers on his neck, I sighed. "He's alive—just unconscious."

"We need him to create the Triangle of Might," Black Scarlett said, anxiously.

"What is that, exactly—a poem or something?" I said.

"It's an ancient prophecy that predicted a change of worlds through the alteration of reflections—the mirrors. The prophecy can be harmful or helpful depending on whose hands it falls into. Gwen has all three mirrors so we need to get them back. Three of us are needed to form the triangle, to call the mirrors into our power. In order for them to come, a chant must be repeated three times by you, me and Sparks right now," she said. "It's called the Triangle of Might; one of strength to bind—that's Sparks, and two identical of power—that's you and me. I can't believe that it happened like that, but it did!"

Black Scarlett was quite educated on the matter. I was impressed at how much she knew. I still couldn't believe that I was having an actual conversation with her, or me rather. In a weird, narcissistic way, I was in awe of myself.

"Now I know what Avari meant," I said. "We have to call for the mirrors."

Black Scarlett nodded. "Yes, but we all have to be awake to say it," she stressed.

Immediately, we both looked down at Sparks, knowing very well that our time was limited.

"Sparks—wake up! Wake up!" I said, tapping his face.

Seconds later, his lips began to move.

"That's right, Sparks. Wake up!" A voice echoed from somewhere behind us.

Black Scarlett and I shared the same sentiments. "Oh no!"

She lifted Sparks' head and cradled it in her lap. "Sparks—we need you," she cried. "Please, we need you!"

I looked up and saw the black robe in the centre of the cave.

"I knew you would come," Gwen said. "The good in you wanted to save your friends. And well . . . here you are." Her tone was bitter and corrosive.

I refrained from answering. Instead, I lowered my head and watched as Sparks' body began to stir.

"What . . . what . . . where am I?" His head flopped from side to side as he tried to comprehend the situation. "Am I really seeing two of you?"

"Yeah—you are," Black Scarlett said. "I'm glad you're okay."

He looked over at me.

"Do you remember me?" I said. "The stubborn one you left at the tunnel?"

"Yeah." His words were slow. "I waited for you . . . but . . . they found me. I'm sorry."

Suddenly, a flash of flame brushed over our heads as Gwen released her venom.

"Get down," I said, ducking.

I watched as she moved towards the ceremonial stand. "None of you are going anywhere. There's no way out."

I covered my head with my hands. "I have an idea but we need to act fast. Take my hands and recite the chant."

With our palms locked in position, our bodies formed a triangle on the floor. Together, the other two began the chant.

"Watch out!" Black Scarlett screamed as another ball of fire came towards us.

We pressed our bodies to the floor. I closed my eyes and dove deep into my mind to channel someone else's fears.

Eyes tightly shut, I let my thoughts venture back to when I was climbing the Tree of Life. I knew in my heart that I possessed a power that allowed me to reach the web safely and help reclaim the forests. I was unstoppable there. I felt genuinely happy knowing that I'd done something good. It was *me* that they needed; Avari confirmed it.

Right now, these people needed me and I wasn't going to let them down. Two versions of me existed in this place, and if I possessed the power to overcome evil, then so did she.

As the others continued, I reached with my mind into Black Scarlett's heart and withdrew the Star of Hope. Without breaking the triangle, I lifted the light from her heart and wrapped it around us, forming a shield.

Just as it appeared, a stream of red fire slammed against the side of it. I looked out behind me and saw Gwen trying to break the barrier. So far, nothing had made it through.

I listened to the words of my friends. Once they registered in my head, I chimed in. We repeated the chant three times over, until all of a sudden the mirrors appeared around us.

When our hands broke apart from one another, the protective wall disappeared. "We have to destroy those two mirrors," I pointed. "The other one is mine to take back."

"NOOO!" Gwen screamed from across the cave.

But before Sparks or Black Scarlett had a chance to move, they were blasted into the air by violent lashes of fire. Each one fell to the ground, landing without strain.

"Scarlett! Sparks!" I cried. Neither one responded. They remained on the ground, in positions unnatural.

"NO! What have you done?!" I turned to face the menace that hunted me.

Gwen's laugh was hideous. Pleased at the outcome, she tossed a ball of fire back and forth between her hands, as if she were playing with it. "Aren't you forgetting one?" she said with a crooked grin.

Then with effortless ease, she wafted towards the ceremonial stand and lifted the black sheet. Beneath it laid the broken body of my precious feline.

"YOU MURDERER!" I wailed.

She smiled at me with sinister intent. "You will never defeat me!"

"HOW DARE YOU!" The anger I had bottled away, burst from my hands in the form of white hot lightning. One after the other, vicious strokes of light flew through the air as I thrust my fury upon her. I didn't know where it was stemming from, but apparently I had powers even without the necklace. I screamed in frustration, hoping that just one of the strikes would finish her off.

Gwen dodged every attack. She jeered incessantly, her voice mocking my every move. I grew weary with every misfire; my heart was sinking. I couldn't understand how someone could be so evil.

As I threw my last strike, I heard the fateful hiss of the Mirrorwalkers' most deadly weapon. Out from behind Gwen's robe, slid the Scarlett King Cobra. Its cold reptilian eyes glared at me as its scaly body slithered along the floor in my direction.

Oh my God! The snake wasn't small, as I had hoped. Its body was a foot wide and at least ten feet long. Its crimson colour made my heart skip a beat.

My gaze didn't break, not even to look for a place to hide. The cobra's eyes told me that it was thirsty for blood—my blood. And running, I figured, would only help its cause.

Then out of nowhere, the Mirrorwalkers appeared. They began to file in behind the cobra, and for a moment I believed I would never make it home.

As they approached, a quiet buzzing appeared in the cave. At first it was soft but then it got louder and louder. My heart began to beat erratically.

'*Be strong, Scarlett—for all of us!*' The words repeated in my head.

To my surprise, hundreds of flying white snakes appeared. I couldn't believe it. I had never seen anything like them before. Each one emitted a gentle glow which reminded me of Avari's light. And I knew at once that they were here to help. Right then and there, my heart began to lift.

They hovered behind me as rows and rows of them gathered, waiting for my signal. They nodded and bowed their tiny heads to me.

Falling into place behind them, were thousands of colourful Robberflies. Leading them into battle was my tiny pink friend from the tunnel. It lowered its head to me in a loyal manner.

My back straightened as my confidence returned.

Looking at the hordes of fearless warriors behind me, I smiled.

"I had an interesting meeting with one of your little Robberflies. I guess I'm their new boss!"

My tone was bold.

"Not for long, my twin. It's too bad I helped you out all those years. And this is how you repay me?"

"Save it, Gwen. That sister stuff doesn't work on me anymore. It died the same day Dad did."

"There are other lives I can take, you know."

"I will stop you—even if I die trying!"

Gwen's stare was heartless. "What about Uncle Frankie—you think he can withstand another stroke?"

I shook my head in disbelief. "You caused that? How could you! He was innocent—he had nothing to do with this!"

"Well, he shouldn't have been messing around with that stone. But you know what my dear sister? The best part came after, when he went absolutely crazy. I can't tell you how much I enjoyed seeing him go to that nursing home." Her lips curled in satisfaction. "Once they sedated him, he just sat there like a vegetable, knowing very well that I was the one who put him there. Sadly, he couldn't say a thing about me and you want to know why? Because no one would have believed him."

My voice was stern and full of contempt. "I will go back and fix all of this!"

"Trust me," she said, "you will not make it out of here alive."

"Just try and stop me!"

"I don't have to—they will," she pointed to her minions. "GET HER!" she ordered.

"ATTACK!" I hollered in return. The space immediately filled with colour as my flying friends enveloped the cave.

Behind the swarm, I retreated. After locating the axe, I ran to pick it up. Holding it securely in my grasp, I suddenly remembered something that Sparks had said—'the fire within their ears'. He was referring to his stash of firecrackers and it gave me an idea. Any concerns I had now were relinquished by my desire to end this fight.

I rushed over to Sparks' backpack and rifled through it, searching for the firecrackers. I dropped the axe and grabbed as many sticks as I could. I then found a box of matches in one of the pockets.

Behind me, the war battled on. The Mirrorwalkers were kept at bay by my new flying comrades. Thank God they had come. I assumed that that was Avari's doing or perhaps, even Habock's.

Gwen's voice tore through the cave. "BE GONE!" she bellowed, and in an instant my allies disappeared into the night.

The Mirrorwalkers reconvened and rallied together as they began to make their way towards me.

I looked around and thought only of what was in my hand. I hoped that what I was about to do would not kill me. The stalactites hung precariously above me but it was too late to think about that. I dropped all but one of the firecrackers. Looking down, I struck the first match on my pants.

I brought the flame to the bottom of the firecracker and quickly threw it into the mass of black. With the speed of a gazelle, I ran in the other direction. I crouched down and covered my ears.

The explosion resonated throughout the cave as a smoky screen coated the air. Terrified cries echoed through the space but all I could do was ignore them. I looked up and saw part of the ceiling crumble. Without hesitation, I ran for the first mirror and picked up the axe.

"This is for Sparks!" With one fell swoop, I smashed the first mirror with the blade. Pieces of my reflection flew across the floor as my inner rage led the destruction.

I glanced back and watched as some of the Mirrorwalkers exploded into nothing. A smile spread along my face when I realized that my plan was working.

Dropping the axe, I returned to the pile of sticks. I grabbed another match and three more firecrackers, lit them all and threw them into the crowd. Again, I kept my distance as the enemy's screams filled the air.

Bang. Bang. Bang.

Good, I thought. *That should keep them busy.* I then ran for the next mirror.

My feet were silenced when a wave of falling rock landed in front of me. The ceiling spears were losing their hold. One by one they crashed all around the cave.

Too bad, Scarlett—you chose this path, I reminded myself. *You have to keep going. You have to end this!* With hurried steps, I dodged past the falling rocks. Quickly, I picked up the axe.

Just as I neared the second mirror, my legs were swept from beneath my body. With a forceful blow, I landed on my chest. My bottom jaw hit the floor hard, causing tears to swell up in my eyes. "Ahh!" I cried. Spots of darkness blurred my vision and I couldn't seem to focus on anything but the pain.

"Is that all you've got, twin? Honestly, I didn't think you'd give up that easily," Gwen boasted above me. I could feel the pull of evil as she moved her fingers along my back.

My head felt dizzy and it seemed as though my circulation was slowing. All of my injuries were coalescing on the ground. Was this how my story was going to end? Was I doomed to die on the dirt floor of this hidden place, where my body would never be found? There was no hand to lift me up this time. No Avari. No Black Scarlett. No Habock. I was truly alone, and the thought of that only saddened me more. I had no idea how I would recover from this.

The beats of my heart were inconsistent and I knew that something was seriously wrong. As I listened to the internal drumming, I knew that time was slowing down for me.

I was so close to destroying the second mirror when my body was struck down. I was now paying for the desperate actions I took.

The enemy leaned into my ear and whispered. "Don't worry—I'll bury you right next to your father. You two can be together in peace."

Then something strange happened. Habock materialized beside me as he stretched out his paw. His fur gently touched my hand. He gazed into my eyes and told me that it wasn't my time yet. His little body beamed with light as Avari appeared behind him. Her soft glow reached into my heart and I could feel her power within me. "Be strong, Scarlett," I heard her say. "Come back to us." They hadn't left me—their spirits were still here.

As I came to, I heard Gwen's voice above me. "I told you that you wouldn't make it out alive. You're not strong enough!"

I salvaged the remaining strength I had as I mentally pulled mysel together. In all of my pain, I connected my mind and body. With a heavy tongue, I spoke. "You're not powerful enough to kill me . . ."

"Oh? We'll just see about that," she answered.

I knew I had very little time to act. As I distracted her with my words my ears focussed on where she was standing.

"You forgot one thing, sis," I said, my voice deceivingly torpid.

"And what's that?" she said, leaning in.

With all my might, I raised the right side of my body and hurled my hand across her chest. "You left a window open!"

She had an odd look in her eyes as if she hadn't expected it. Then she staggered away as I tenderly lifted myself off of the ground.

I watched her carefully as she pulled her hand away. Blood now oozed from beneath the robe and descended onto the floor.

"You chose a human body—that made you vulnerable," I said, holding the bloodied axe.

Behind me, all the remaining Mirrorwalkers screamed in pain as their connection to the Leader disintegrated.

Time was of the essence though, I had to move on. With the axe in tow, I carefully made my way through falling rock towards the second mirror. Destroying it was next on my itinerary.

When I approached, I took a deep breath and gave a hearty swing. The mirror shattered into pieces as each fragment fell to the ground. "That was for Black Scarlett."

I could hear Gwen gasping for air as the blood gushed from her system. Normally, I would have fainted at the sight of such a thing, but this I needed to see. I looked back and saw her collapse onto her knees.

From the far side of the cave, came the Scarlett King Cobra. It crawled raggedly along the floor until it reached its commander. It coiled loosely at the base of her feet as if it were preparing to sleep. It too, had been severely wounded.

Gwen looked up at me, her skin now crumbling.

"You will never get the chance to do this to anyone else. Your time here is done," I said.

I turned and sidestepped piles of cascading rock as I headed for the bodies of my friends. Feeling their pain, I knelt down beside them. "I hope we meet again," I said, touching their hands. I could barely see through the tears in my eyes.

I then stood and moved towards the stand in the centre of the cave. Softly, I rested my head on Habock's body and cried. "I'm sorry I couldn't save you. I'm so sorry, Habock. Please forgive me." I petted his still body and kissed his furry head.

My moment of sorrow was suddenly broken when a wave of fire brushed past my shoulders, nearly hitting me. I grabbed my chest in surprise.

Looking back, I saw Gwen's arm stretched out in front of her. She had tried one last time to kill me.

"You will never be rid of me! NEVER!" she sneered.

Then, in an unexpected turn, her body caught fire and exploded into the air as a firecracker erupted by her feet. I covered Habock's body with my own as the blast blanketed the space behind us.

As smoke once again began to fill the cave, I looked back and saw Sparks fall onto the ground. With his last breath, he'd thrown the firecracker to protect me. And now the life in him was gone.

"Thank you, Sparks." My words were solemn. "You saved my life."

Gazing down at Habock's body, I wept. "Goodbye my friend." I wrapped him inside the black fabric and turned to leave. My heart was tearing from all sides.

I was jolted out of my sobs when the cave began to shake, violently. Stalactites crashed all around me as the ceiling and walls toppled and tumbled. With the Leader's demise, came the demolition of the cave. Soon, everything in it would be buried beneath the rubble.

As pieces of my surroundings tore about recklessly, I knew that the time had come to leave. I had to get out of the cave fast, before I too, got buried inside of it.

With the axe firmly in my hand, I ran towards the third mirror, carrying all of my wounds with me. I was disheartened when all I saw was my own reflection. Somehow I had made it out alive, but my lone survival saddened me.

With the burden of knowledge I had gained, I placed half of my body into the mirror. Then carefully, I reeled the other half into the frame. My ears were deafened by the sounds of destruction but now I was encapsulated within the mirror's safety.

Darkness took my vision. Solitude took my body.

And from there I travelled to a place called home.

HOME IS WHERE THE CAT IS

F I HAD to choose three words to describe my experience, I would use: magical, educational and humbling. To see another time was one thing but to *be* in another time was downright difficult. I hadn't realized what a ride I was in for.

In the end, I understood the true meaning of friendship, betrayal and growth. I knew that my relationships could be mended and that lives could be saved. I was taken to the future to learn a lesson, and brought back to the past to prove it.

I was beginning to feel like a pro: climbing, falling, jumping, leaping, crying, landing. Here I was again, falling into something. But this time I landed on my feet.

It seemed as though I had been away for years and yet in reality it was only one day, less than one day to be accurate. I had so many questions still and I wondered whether I'd ever find anyone to explain them. That point aside, I was finally home inside the attic. Everything was just as I had left it: unorganized and messy, boxes everywhere. *Good—great!*

Looking down, I realized that my wounds had disappeared. My cuts and scrapes had faded and I was left now with only one scar.

With my hand over my heart, I turned to face the mirror. The axe was still gripped tightly between my fingers.

"Goodbye everyone." I lifted my arms and just as I was ready to swing, an image appeared in front of me. A cold, ghostly face hovered over a cloaked body. I shuddered when I recognized who it was: Gwen.

Two red, snake-like eyes watched me from the other side of the mirror. "You will never be rid of me—you'll see!"

Her voice taunted me, as did her entire existence. It was too late, though. I'd had enough. The time to end this was now. With one final infuriated blow, I smashed the mirror into pieces. "That one was for Habock." I dropped the axe and lowered my head to cry.

"Wow—you're still up here. I gotta say kiddo, you did a great job!" a voice came from behind me.

I knew that voice. Instantly, I turned. "DAD!" I screamed, as I raced across the attic floor. I practically knocked him over as I thrust my arms around him. "You're here! I'm so happy—you have no idea how happy I am right now. No idea!"

"Scarlett—what's gotten into you?" he smiled.

"Well, it's been so long since I've seen you . . . and then I lost you . . ."

"Whoa—where exactly did I go?" he said, lifting my chin. "Sweetie—why are you crying?"

With the sleeve of my coat, I brushed away my tears. As much as I wanted to tell him about my adventure, I knew that I couldn't. "I'm just so glad to see you—is that such a crime?"

"Not at all, kiddo. Not at all. But I do have a question, why are you wearing a coat—it's hot outside."

I had completely forgotten that I was wearing black Scarlett's clothes. "Oh, this old thing? I found it in one of the boxes," I said, nonchalantly.

"Oh, okay. Listen, why don't you come downstairs, it's almost dinner time. Your mother made meatloaf—your favourite," he laughed.

My stomach did a back flip. I may have learned many things in the future, but adapting my appetite wasn't one of them. Still, I had to at least try to be agreeable. "Okay, Dad, but first I have to . . ." My sentence came to a halt when I gazed down at the ground and saw that the axe was not there. When I looked back at the mirror—it was gone, too. Not just broken, but gone altogether. "Hey, where did the mirror go?"

"What mirror?" he said.

"You know, the one with the lion's feet?"

"Scarlett, what are you talking about? There's no mirror up here."

"Really? I could have sworn that I saw . . ."

"Okay, kiddo. Stop stalling. I know you don't like meatloaf, but you need to come down and eat something," he said, heading towards the attic door.

"But what about Gwen—I thought she was at soccer practice."

Well, that stopped him. My father walked back to me and placed his hand on my forehead. "Are you feeling okay?"

"Yeah—*why?*"

"Um . . . wasn't Gwen the name of your imaginary friend when you were a kid?"

Oh my God—is that what they thought? How was that possible? I was sent back from the future with a full memory of what had happened, except now I had no sister. That was going to take some time getting used to.

"You know what—I'll be right down," I said, trying to hide my disillusion.

"Are you sure you're okay?"

I nodded.

He left my side and climbed down the ladder.

I looked around the room and sighed. I'd been through so much in one day. What I needed was some time to unwind and let it all soak in.

I wandered over to the window and lifted my eyes to the moon. "Thank you for believing in me, Avari . . . I mean, Mom." I said. "I don't know if you can hear me or not but I couldn't have done it without your help."

I knew that after talking with Avari inside Velvet Elm, she represented my mother. It was mostly her green eyes that gave it away but her voice and tenderness also helped. There was no denying what Avari truly meant to me.

As I turned away, I heard a soft voice answer. "You're welcome."

A huge grin spread across my face when she spoke. It was Avari, I didn't have to look back to know.

My smile disappeared though when I remembered what happened to Habock. I knew it would take time for me to recover from his loss. Especially since he'd been in the house since I was a baby. I loved him so much.

There was nothing else for me to do but move on. With that last thought, I headed for the attic door. I stepped through the opening and descended down the ladder. Then, after taking one final look around, I closed the door to my futuristic journey.

The sounds of my parent's voices became clearer as I lumbered down the stairs. I wasn't in the mood to talk, not after what I'd been through. Seeing my father was the only saving grace right now. Thank goodness he was here but I had to keep it that way. I needed to steer him away from danger.

When I entered the kitchen, I saw my mother standing in front of the oven. "Scarlett, there you are. You've been up in the attic all day; we thought you got lost," she giggled. "Hey, did you find Grandpa's long underwear?"

The first thing I noticed was her colour: it had returned. And so had her personality; her humour was endearing.

"Mom—I missed you." I veered across the floor and squeezed her.

"Missed me? What are you talking about?"

"Oh . . . it's a long story, I guess. I'll tell you some other time. I'm just glad that both you and Dad are here right now."

"Well, where else would we be?"

I didn't answer. I was distracted by the settings on the dinner table. "How come there are five plates? Who else is eating?"

"Your uncle is here . . ."

"Uncle Frankie? I thought he was in the nursing home."

Just then, my uncle appeared in the doorway. "Hey Scarlett—how's my favourite niece? Give me five," he said, stretching out his hands.

I pushed them aside and hugged him.

Apparently I was scaring my family.

"Scarlett's hugging everyone today—go with it," my mother said.

"Now, what's this I hear about me in a nursing home? You're not sending me away just yet, are you?" he smiled.

I stared at him but saw no signs of a weakened man. If there were symptoms, I couldn't see them. He seemed strong and enthusiastic—like the man he was before the stroke.

"Because," he continued, "I really should tell my patients that I'm leaving."

"What are you talking about, Uncle Frankie? *What* patients?"

My mother had a strange look on her face. "Scarlett—you know that your uncle is a vet. Goodness, I'm starting to worry about you."

"A vet? Really?" I questioned him. "I mean . . . of course you're a vet . . . I knew that," I said, trying to smooth over my surprise.

The doorbell rang as I stood there sorting out my confusion.

"Scarlett—why don't you get that," my mother said.

I obliged. I left the room and headed for the front door. My hear
fluttered when I opened it. "Sparks . . . I mean . . . Ainsley!" I gushed.

"Hi, Scar."

"What are you doing here?"

"Your folks invited me over for dinner."

I just about choked on my own words. "What? Sorry—that didn't
come out right. I meant *WHAT?*"

"Scarlett," my mother yelled from the kitchen, "the polite thing is to
invite the boy in."

Okay, now I was freaking out. *Wasn't this the same day I left when I went to
the future? Why is everyone acting so different?* But then I remembered—Gwen
no longer existed in this time. Uncle Frankie wasn't in a nursing home
because Gwen wasn't around to put him there. He never found the broken
Seeing stone because it didn't exist in the house.

As for Sparks, Gwen wasn't here to tarnish his good name. He was just
some nice guy from school, standing in my doorway. A guy I might add,
that my parents seemed to like.

Then something jogged my memory. I remembered the agreement that
Habock and I made before we left for the future. He said that he would
help me out with my parents. How was that possible, though—he never
made it back. For a moment, my thoughts turned sour, but I had to remind
myself that my father was here and well.

"Hey, kiddo," he called from the kitchen. "I was thinking of getting
take-out the night of your party. How does pizza sound?"

Without thinking, I dashed back into the kitchen screaming. "No! No
pizza! No take-out!"

Everyone was staring at me, and who could blame them, I was acting
like a lunatic.

"Sorry, what I meant . . . was that . . . I'd rather have them deliver."

"Okay, if that's what you want," my father said, leaving the room.

My uncle opened the back door as Odin came barrelling through the
hallway into the kitchen.

"Odin—there's my boy!" I said, reaching out to hug him. I was glad
to be back in this time, where my dog now remembered me. I knelt down
and scratched his back.

"How's Adonis?" I said. Quickly, I cupped my hand over my mouth. I
was shocked at my own words.

"Who's Adonis?" my uncle asked, looking around the room.

"I don't know," my mother said. "Sweetie—who's Adonis?"

I back peddled as fast as I could. "Oh . . . nobody. No one."

My father's voice carried from the next room. "Well—I don't know who that is, Scarlett, but I do know who this is," he said, entering the kitchen with a bundle in his arms. "Happy birthday, kiddo—we got you an early birthday present." The bundle moved and a black-tipped head was exposed.

I took one look and then broke into tears. "Oh, Dad—he's beautiful!"

Tucked within his arms and looking back at me, was Habock.

Gently, he handed him to me as I wrapped my arms around his furry feline body. "You came back to me," I whispered into his ears.

My heart was elated. The wish I had made, was granted: my family was back together. *Thank you, Avari.*

Everyone stood around me, waiting to pet him.

"It's funny, he showed up at my clinic one night with no collar, no tags, no owner," Frankie said.

"And when your uncle called to tell us, we knew that it was meant to be," my mother swooned.

"Yeah, he's quite the talker," Frankie smiled. "Hey, wait a minute . . . I never called you guys. How did you find out?"

My parents looked at one another and shrugged. "That's odd," my father said, "because I remember getting a phone call . . ."

I never heard the rest of that sentence. I simply looked at Habock and shook my head. I couldn't help but laugh.

He placed his paw in front of his mouth. "Shhh . . ." he whispered. Then with a playful grin, he winked.

And I knew right there, that the next stage of our journey was about to begin.

ABOUT THE AUTHOR

ARA BARTLEY HAS always been interested in animals, so it comes as no surprise that her world is surrounded by them in both her life and imagination.

She has a bachelor's degree in Biology/Earth Science, a post-graduate diploma in Geographic Information Systems and a master's degree in Vertebrate Paleontology. In the spring of 2002, she began writing her first novel, *The Siamese Mummy* while on a dig for fossils in Kansas. The book was later released in 2006.

Kara is also the author of *The Unearthlings* and *Call of Adhara*. She lives in Niagara Falls with her three Siamese cats—one of which is terribly naughty. Her horse, Dapplynn, is her biggest companion and anxiously awaits the day that she too will have a guest appearance in one of her mother's books.

ABOUT THE ILLUSTRATOR

TAMMY DUNLAVEY GREW up in North East, Pennsylvania with the innate ability to draw. When it came to education, Tammy chose science over art, as science offered her a path untaken.

In August of 2001, Tammy was diagnosed with Multiple sclerosis. In light of her medical challenges, she continued on and graduated with a master's degree in Invertebrate Paleontology.

Although Tammy has returned to her artistic roots, she finds that paleontology often appears within her art. Her journey with MS has also played a significant role in her work as her health experiences are well expressed in her creativity.

She is inspired by her son Keegan, her daughter Ellen and her granddaughter Molly-Jane. Her extended family of four-legged pets also provide her with much amusement and love.

THE PALEO TWINS

AMMY AND I first met at grad school in the fall of 2002. The first thing I remember her saying to me was, "Oh—*she* must be the Vertebrate Palaeontologist!" From that moment on, we were friends.

We shared an office in the geology department at the University at Buffalo where Tammy studied Invertebrate paleontology and I studied Vertebrate paleontology. Two rival scientists with a common love of fossils and animal history. Who would have known?

Throughout our studies, we talked and travelled. At school we were given the name 'The Paleo Twins' and to our delight, it stuck. Tammy became my sister and for the years we spent in that office, I felt like I had family.

I soon found out that my twin had an amazing flare for artistry, whereas I began to succumb to the creativeness of words. Two scientists turned artists, I'm sure our professors are still scratching their heads.

It was through school that we met as friends but it was paleontology that brought us together as artists.

Our support for one another transcended our education as Tammy and I joined forces once again for this novel. She is the illustrator behind the words and I am the storyteller behind the pictures.

Hopefully, this will not be our last creative endeavour.

CPSIA information can be obtained
at www.ICGtesting.com
Printed in the USA
FSHW011409120419
57199FS